THREE FLAMES

ALSO BY ALAN LIGHTMAN

FICTION
Mr g
Ghost
Reunion
The Diagnosis
Good Benito
Einstein's Dreams

NONFICTION
Searching for Stars on an Island in Maine
In Praise of Wasting Time
Screening Room
The Accidental Universe
A Sense of the Mysterious
Dance for Two
The Discoveries: Great Breakthroughs in
20th Century Science
Origins: The Lives and Worlds of Modern Cosmologists
Time for the Stars
Ancient Light: Our Changing View of the Universe

POETRY
Song of Two Worlds

THREE FLAMES

A Novel

Alan Lightman

COUNTERPOINT

BERKELEY, CALIFORNIA

Copyright © 2019 by Alan Lightman
First hardcover edition: 2019

An earlier version of the chapter "Ryna" first appeared in *Daily Lit* magazine under the title "Reprisals." An earlier version of the chapter "Pich" first appeared in *Consequence* magazine.

Library of Congress Cataloging-in-Publication Data
Names: Lightman, Alan P., 1948– author.
Title: Three flames : a novel / Alan Lightman.
Description: First hardcover edition. | Berkeley, California : Counterpoint, 2019.
Identifiers: LCCN 2018057994 | ISBN 9781640092280
Subjects: LCSH: Cambodia—History—Fiction.
Classification: LCC PS3562.I45397 T47 2019 | DDC 813/.54—dc23
LC record available at https://lccn.loc.gov/2018057994

Jacket design by Jaya Miceli
Book design by Wah-Ming Chang

COUNTERPOINT
2560 Ninth Street, Suite 318
Berkeley, CA 94710
www.counterpointpress.com

Printed in the United States of America
Distributed by Publishers Group West

10 9 8 7 6 5 4 3 2 1

This book is dedicated to the strong and courageous young women of the Harpswell Foundation.

Contents

THREE FLAMES

RYNA

~

(2012)

Ryna had just finished putting a quarter kilo of pork and a half dozen rambutan into her burlap shopping bag, wondering if her husband would scold her for spending too much, when she saw the man who had murdered her father. At first she wasn't sure. She hadn't seen the man for thirty-three years, since she was twelve years old, and he was now whitened and bent over and barely able to support his skinny body with a walking stick. But he had the same crooked mouth and angular cheeks that she remembered, the same mole above his left eye, and as she studied him from three stalls away, she became more and more certain. Many times over the years since the war, she had imagined what she would do if she ever saw him again. What she had most wished for was some catastrophe to permanently separate him from his family, as had happened to her family, or for him to be stricken with cancer and die a slow and painful death.

That evening, after her husband had finished eating his dinner, Ryna said to him, "I think I saw Touch Pheng in the market this morning." The smell of the pork blended with the odor of mildew, always present during the rainy season, when nothing could be kept dry.

"Who?" said Pich, wiping his mouth.

"The commander of the camp at Sopheak Mongkol."

She looked over at Pich through the dim yellow light and tried to read his expression. The one room of the house was lit only by a single bulb, which dangled from wires that ran along the tin roof, down a wall made of packed palm leaves, around the two storage bags of corn and rice, and finally to a car battery in the corner.

"Why are you talking about that?" said Pich, annoyed. "And anyway, how do you know it was him? It's been so many years."

"Do you remember when I saw Cousin Mala after forty years? You didn't believe me then either."

Pich didn't bother replying. He was sharpening the blade of his plow, which he would need to finish

4

preparing his fields for planting. Sharpening blades was their son Kamal's job, but Kamal was out as usual, drinking cheap wine in the rain with his friends.

Pich stood and began putting his tools away. He was not much taller than his wife and almost as thin, with fleshy lips, perpetually bloodshot eyes, and a scar on his cheek where he'd been gored by a neighbor's ox. Now the rain was pinging like gunshots on the tin roof, causing the two oxen under the house to shuffle nervously. Ryna could look down between the bamboo poles of the floor and see their shadowy forms fidgeting below.

"What should we do?" said Ryna.

"What's there to do? Why do you want to think about such a useless thing? It's a waste of time. And tomorrow don't buy any rambutan." Pich was always especially unpleasant the day after he'd spent the night with Lakhena.

"I am doing, I don't yet know what."

"What is silly *Mae Wea* going to do?"

"Something." Unsettled, Ryna sat down next to Thida, her eldest daughter, who began brushing her mother's hair. At age sixteen, Thida had gone to Phnom Penh to work off a family debt. She'd been back home for a year, eating regularly, but her wrists were still smaller than the thickness of a cucumber, and she sometimes began screaming in the middle of the night. Their middle daughter, Nita, Pich had married off at age sixteen to a traveling rubber mer-chant, who promptly deposited his new wife for safe-keeping with his aunt on the far side of Battambang Province. But at least Ryna still had her youngest daughter, Sreypov, her *mi-oun*, still in school at Ryna's fierce insistence. She would give her life to protect Sreypov. Ryna looked over at her youngest daughter, in the corner, reading one of her schoolbooks. Srey-pov, although only fourteen, had her own mind and wrote poetry. She was the fire in the family.

Ryna closed her eyes, hoping the long brush-strokes would calm her. Her jet-black hair fell to the middle of her back. Despite her age, she was still an attractive woman, with a slender body and a sympa-thetic mouth, but her skin had become worn with the heat and the life on the farm, and deep grooves spread out from the corners of her eyes. One could see the Chinese blood on her father's side, as her nose was more narrow and her skin lighter than pure Khmer.

"I've had enough of silly talk for the day," said Pich. "I'm getting old. And tomorrow is almost here." With-out bothering to take off his sweaty shirt, he lay down on his sleeping mat. Almost immediately, Sreypov and Thida disappeared behind the dangling sheet that parti-tioned off the tiny area where they undressed and slept.

Once the house had grown silent, Ryna began brooding again about Touch Pheng, and her hands started to shake. She would do something horrible to him. She walked to the corner of the room where the family said prayers for their ancestors. On a table were candles, bits of colored string, photographs of Pich's parents and grandparents and of Ryna's mother and two grandmothers. Ryna possessed only a single picture of her father, which she kept safe in a small metal box. Now she lit a candle and took out the photograph, stained and curled around the edges. Here her father was a young man, perhaps twenty-five years old, handsome and sweet. In her mind, she could see the moonless night he was killed, she could see the red glow of the hand-rolled cigarettes of the Khmer Rouge soldiers as they sat under a tree, she could hear their voices as they came to her father's bunkhouse and called him out along with two other men who had all tried to escape to find missing members of their families. "We are moving you to another camp," said Touch Pheng, a phrase whose meaning all understood. She could hear the commander's raspy and arrogant voice. She had seen him order the executions of people before, as easily as if he were swatting mosquitoes. The cadres carried shovels and ropes. Ryna looked at the photograph and said a prayer for her father. Inexplicably, she began thinking of the time they had gone together to Phnom Penh when she was a little girl and sat on the grass below the great monument celebrating the departure of the French. Ryna had never seen a city. Amid the noisy crush of buildings and people flying by on their cycles and motos, her father sat quietly humming a song to her. Somewhere, in the distance, she heard Pich snoring. Ryna put a cupful of sticky rice sweetened with palm sugar on the sleeping mats of each of her children, as she had done for years, and lay down.

After a night of tossing and turning, Ryna rose before dawn, climbed barefoot down the rickety wooden ladder to the ground, and began preparing breakfast and lunch in the little shed that served as the kitchen, ten meters from the house. Thida had gotten up even earlier to start the wood fire. Until harvest, their food was limited, but Ryna could still season it with garlic and ginger. A little later, Ryna roused Pich and Kamal, who ate their rice and bits of dried fish in the dark without speaking. Afterward, the men loaded up the oxcart with sacks of rice seed and tools and left for the farm.

When she and Thida had finished cleaning the dishes, Ryna swept the floor and dusted the tables and the sleeping mats and the walls. It was 8 a.m., time for the market. She gathered up food scraps for the oxen and went down the ladder again to the ground. Passing the kitchen shed, she caught sight of the pork knife and put it in her shopping bag.

The market was always a barrage of color and sound, offering a thousand distractions, but this morning Ryna

walked purposefully past the oranges and the red rambutan, the lavender and magenta fabrics, the screaming
half-naked children and the chickens darting down the
muddy path between the stalls, until she spotted the
man standing near the covered stall that sold mangoes.
She approached him as closely as she dared and got a
good look, much better than the day before. She even
heard him speak, asking how much he owed for a half
dozen mangoes. Was it the voice she remembered? It
was the tired voice of an old man. After a minute, he
seemed to feel her eyes and returned her gaze. They
stared at each other for a few uncomfortable moments.
She gripped the handle of the knife in her bag. Then
the man looked away and hobbled to the next stall. She
would not approach him now, not today.

It was still early in the morning and already so hot
that the sweat had soaked through Ryna's shirt. She
nodded to several people she knew and bowed to a
procession of monks in saffron robes, walking through
the muddy ruts left by the oxcarts. When she passed
the house of her best friend, Makara, she waited a few
moments at the wire fence. But Makara wasn't there.

Although Ryna had lived in this village for nearly
thirty years, only in the last few had she felt that she
might begin to belong. This was her husband's provin-
cial home, not hers. Her birth village was in Pursat. She
hadn't returned there since that frightening morning

a lifetime ago when the young soldiers appeared and dragged everyone off to the camps. Only two years after the Khmer Rouge regime ended, when Ryna was fourteen, her mother had died from gangrene, later her sister. Without any parents, Ryna was taken into the household of her uncle, who arranged for her to marry Pich. She knew nothing of Pich or his village. At first, she had thoughts about going to school, but Pich put her to work on the family farm, and then the children began. After the birth of Thida, when Ryna had been ill with pneumonia, Pich sat by her side day and night putting wet rags on her cheeks and massaging her back. He did the same when she was sick with dengue fever. Over the years, she and Pich had grown accustomed to living with each other. Slowly, she'd made friends in the village, at the funerals and the weddings.

Thirty years. All of Ryna's uncles and aunts had passed away and now seemed like the shadows of vanishing dreams. The only remaining link to her village in Pursat was her childhood friend Makara, who, upon marriage, had refused to share a sleeping mat with her husband until he agreed to live in the same village as Ryna. Every Sunday for the last twenty-five years, she and Makara walked arm in arm by the river, escaping for a few precious hours their household obligations and their husbands. Makara was her lifeline. Makara was her soul mate. She laughed with Makara.

It was Makara who had first discovered that Ryna's husband was sleeping with Lakhena. Half the married men in the village had girlfriends, but few of them lived nearby. "I'm so sorry, dear sister," she told Ryna, and hugged her. When Ryna confronted Pich about the affair, he said only: "It's none of your business." Since then, a year ago, Pich had been spending one night a week with Lakhena. Every month, Lakhena sent little gifts to Ryna's children, pieces of fruit and bits of colored fabric, delivered by a toothless former monk. Ryna would always throw the gifts into the river. Pich called Lakhena his *bropun jong*, his second wife, but Ryna and her friends called her a *srey somphoeung*, a slut.

That night, after the second time she had seen Touch Pheng in the market, Ryna could hardly close her eyes. It was hot, without any breezes, and she was thinking about the man. She saw him covered with blood, swaggering about their village. Then she was a child, back in the camp, eating grasshoppers and crickets and anything she could find, digging canals in the mud with her fingers, hungry, always hungry, trying to catch sight of her father and little brother and sister.

The following morning, the whitened old man with the crooked mouth was not at the market. Nor the morning after that. A week later, Ryna spotted him again, standing in front of some children playing in the mud near several crates of oranges. This time, she walked straight up to him. "Are you Touch Pheng?" she asked. He seemed to lean more heavily on his stick. "Do you know who I am?" said Ryna, her voice not as confident as before. He shook his head no. He smelled of tobacco. "Were you in Sopheak Mongkol during the Pol Pot time?" whispered Ryna. The man said nothing, but she could see something cross his face. Slowly, he turned around on his cane, putting his stooped back toward her.

On her way home, Ryna stopped at Makara's house. Today, Makara was home. "The man who killed my father," said Ryna. "He's alive. I saw him here, in the village."

Makara stopped feeding her chickens and looked up. Over the years, she had lost a couple of teeth and gained weight, but she still had her broad and welcoming face. "When?"

"Ten days ago."

"Really! Why didn't you tell me? What are you going to do? The police won't do anything."

"I know. I haven't decided what I'm going to do."

"But you are doing something," said Makara. "Those killers should be brought to justice. They should suffer. You owe it to your father." She put her arm around Ryna. "I'll tell Sayon. He knows about these things. He'll tell you what you can do. Where's this man living? Can you show him to me?"

"I don't . . ." Ryna found herself suddenly frightened. She needed time to think. "I'm not sure where he lives."

"Sister, this is your chance to have courage. If I could get the soldiers who murdered my uncle and sister . . ." Makara gently patted Ryna's back. "Just tell Sayon when you're ready."

In the following weeks, Ryna saw Touch Pheng several more times at the market. They would stare at each other from a distance, then go about their business. She noticed that the old man was always alone. And as he limped from one stall to the next on his stick, he seemed half in the grave.

The new rice shoots were coming up now, several centimeters tall, close packed and velvety and intensely yellow-green in color. Every afternoon, Ryna spent hours on the farm picking out the invading snails, one by one, and dropping them in a bucket. Soon it would be time for transplanting. Pich went out to drink several nights a week, sneaking five-hundred-riel notes from the envelope under his sleeping mat. In the wee hours of the morning he would call up to Ryna, too drunk to climb the ladder without her help.

After a stifling night in mid-June, Ryna took the photograph of her father from its safe place in the metal box and, for the first time in years, carried it out of the house. When she saw Touch Pheng at the market that morning, she gingerly pulled the picture from her pocket and held it in front of his face. "This was my father," she said. He looked at the photo without speaking. Then he took some sugarcane and rambutan from his basket and held it out to her. "No," she said. But as she turned to go home, he slipped the food into her shopping bag and hobbled away. She threw his food to the ground.

Now Ryna was certain that the old man was Touch Pheng. That evening, while she and Pich were listening to their radio, she wanted to tell her husband about her meetings with Touch Pheng. She wanted Pich to hold her and talk sweetly to her, as he had done when they first married. But she could not make the words come out of her mouth. For years, her husband had acted as if the Pol Pot time had never occurred, although he himself had lost an uncle and two aunts. There were other things he would not discuss as well. Something terrible had happened to his brother, before the Pol Pot time. When they first married, Ryna told Pich all the horrors she had witnessed in her camp—seeing an old man hung upside down from his ankles because he had complained about his thin soup; her little brother dying of starvation; her pretty sixteen-year-old sister Lina snatched up by one of the Khmer Rouge officers and

used every night in his hut; the pile of fresh bodies with slit throats that she stumbled upon in the
bushes one day. And the murder of her father. Pich
had listened and nodded and said, "We will not speak
of this again."

In the fields, in the afternoons, Ryna found herself remembering things about her father that she
thought had been lost to the years and the hardships
of life. She remembered that she would sit on his lap
while he told her the story "Grandma and Rabbit," in
which the mischievous rabbit ate all of Grandma's bananas. When she got older, he told her stories from
other parts of the world, stories she told to her own
children years later. She remembered that when he
would come home after being gone for weeks with
some Chinese businessmen, he would bring a maroon
woven bag from which he would happily pull beautiful carved hairbrushes and strange-tasting spices
and fabrics. He once gave her a turquoise silk scarf
decorated with apsara dancers, and she now remembered the precise moment, his hands touching her
shoulders, the view of pink bougainvillea outside the
half-open window. She remembered that he would
give her a foot massage before bed. Ryna thought of
these things as she worked her trowel into the mud
and scooped up the young rice plants to be replanted
in the adjacent fields. Each fist-size chunk of mud and

rice shoots, a miniature island of dense yellow-green trees, she painstakingly carried to the new field and buried in the mud under the water. She remembered his laugh. She remembered that she was his favorite child. She remembered that he called her his *svay pa-em*, his sweet mango.

In the evenings, as they unrolled the mosquito nets, she told her daughters these fragments of memories. She told them of the places her father had traveled, and they played games, guessing the clothing and foods of faraway peoples and lands. "Grandfather seems so different from Father," said Sreypov. "You must have loved him very much." "Yes," said Ryna. "I wish I could see him," said Sreypov. "I wish he was here. I hope he is not sad in his new life with the spirits." "I hope so too," said Ryna. "Put your hand on my shoulder, *Mae*," said Sreypov. "Why?" "I will imagine it is Grandfather's hand."

One morning as Ryna was leaving her house to take rice to the monks, Makara's husband rode up on his moto. Sayon was a tall man whose hands were always clean despite his work in the fields. "I am offering my help with this killer," he said. "What have you decided to do?"

"I'm not sure," said Ryna.

"You shouldn't wait," said Sayon. "These KR killers don't stay in one place long. There are thousands of them among us. They think they're invisible, like fleas on an ox's back."

"I'm planning something," said Ryna.

"I can do it for you," said Sayon. "Or have a friend do it."

"What would you do?"

"It's easy. We watch him. We get him at night, on the road."

"You kill him?"

"Do you really want to know? We don't kill him. We beat him with a bat until all of his bones are broken. That way, he suffers more." He put the kickstand down on his moto and walked close to Ryna. "Don't you want revenge?" he said in a gentle voice.

"Yes. But the bat . . ."

"These killers have to pay. And you owe it to the memory of your father. Can you tell me his name? Can you show me where he is?"

"I'll let you know," said Ryna. She felt nauseated again, like the first morning she'd seen Touch Pheng. "Not now. I'll let you know."

"Don't wait too long," said Sayon. He patted her shoulder and drove away.

That afternoon, Ryna prepared dinner for her family earlier than usual. Makara had given her a chicken. It fluttered and squawked when Ryna held her knife against its neck. As she slit its throat, she noticed how easily the blade cut through the muscles and flesh. Almost in a trance, she watched the blood drip drop by drop to the ground.

Ryna didn't see Touch Pheng again until the middle of July. He was sitting in a plastic chair underneath the awning of the shop that sold *sleuk bas* and cabbage, and he appeared to be dozing. Without speaking, she walked close to him and just stood staring. She realized that she didn't know what she would do from one moment to the next. She was trying to make his face change into the face of the arrogant young Khmer Rouge officer. She remembered that other face well, but this was the face of an old man. Yet it was also the same.

"My name is Ryna," she said finally. She was surprised at the sound of her own voice. He opened his eyes and nodded. "Are you here by yourself?" she asked.

"Yes," he said, and reached for his stick. It was the first time he had spoken to her. In her mind, she saw him lying on a dark road, broken and bleeding to death.

She hesitated. "Do you have a family?"

He leaned forward on his stick and squinted with milky eyes at the crowd of people moving among the covered food stalls. His forehead glistened with sweat. "My wife died ten years ago," he said. "My children live in Vietnam." He stopped and began coughing. "I don't want to live in Vietnam. The Vietnamese are cheaters and liars."

"May I ask *Ta* what brings him to Praek Banan?"

"I am visiting the daughter of a cousin," said the old man. "For a few months. Then I'll go." He sat back in the chair. "And you? *Neang* must live here?"

"Yes, I have lived in this village for thirty years," said Ryna.

"Are you married?"

"I have a husband and four children."

"You have good luck," said the old man.

In the many scenarios that Ryna had rehearsed in her mind over the last couple of months, she had not imagined such a conversation.

Ryna began taking the photograph of her father with her every time she went to the market. She did not show the picture to Touch Pheng again, or even take it out of her pocket, but she wanted it with her when she saw him. Once a week, she and Touch Pheng would have bits of conversation. A few sentences. He never said much. And she, even less. One morning outside of a new stall that sold used tires hanging from the roof like giant black fruit, Touch Pheng confided that his favorite son had mechanical skill and had secured a job repairing motos. "But he married badly," said the old man, shaking his head, "and is always arguing with his wife. What can I do?" He told Ryna that he had seven grandchildren. On another occasion, as he leaned on his stick and picked at the mole over his eye, he mentioned that for many years now he had been moving from one province to another every few months, living with cousins. "I come and I go, I come and I go. What is an old man to do? I'm lucky to be alive."

Yes, he's lucky to be alive, Ryna thought to herself. Especially when so many had died at his orders. Her father. Her father. What Ryna wanted was for the old man to revert to his younger self, the swaggering killer she remembered, and stop pretending to be someone else. Then, she would know what to do. Over and over, she went through the scenes she remembered. She hated talking to this ancient version of that killer. Yet she found herself doing so. One day, she told him that Kamal was beginning to look for a wife. They were sitting next to a stall that sold chickens. She told him that her daughter Nita was pregnant and might be coming home to live with her and Pich, arriving soon, in early September, in time for the Pchum Ben holidays.

That afternoon, as she was washing the family's clothes in the river, Ryna realized that she had confided far too much in Touch Pheng. How could she have revealed such personal things about herself and her family to that killer? He might not look like the man she remembered, but he was that man. She felt disgusted with herself and scraped a shirt against the cleaning rock harder and harder until it was ripped to shreds and her fingers were bleeding.

She remembered more things of her father, small things. She remembered that his hands were soft and delicate, unlike the hands of Pich.

As she remembered, everyday life was developing a strangeness she'd not experienced before. One morning on her way to the market, she stopped at the little compound next to the pagoda, where the monks slept on straw mats, and listened to their chanting. For ten minutes, she stared at the red-toothed old women chewing on betel leaves under the shade of an acacia tree. For a week, she sat with a friend's fifteen-year-old son who was dying of tuberculosis, watched as he gasped for air and clawed at the pus-filled lesions on his back. At his cremation ceremony, she suddenly began weeping and couldn't stop until evening.

Late one night at the end of July, Makara called from the bottom of the ladder, seeking asylum from her husband. Sayon had beaten her before, but that night Makara seemed particularly terrified, and she had dark blue bruises on her face and a bleeding mouth. After Makara had come up into the house, Ryna leaned down to Pich, half asleep, and said, "If *Ouv Wea* ever hits me like that, I'll be gone in the morning, and he is never going to find me." "Watch your tongue," said Pich, roused from his sleep. "You are the one who needs to watch out," screamed Ryna, surprised at her anger, and suddenly she had a memory of her sister Lina in the camp, beaten so badly she couldn't walk. Ryna took Makara behind the curtain into her daughters' tiny space, and the four of them slept on the mats side by side. The next morning, Makara rose at dawn without speaking and went home to her husband.

At the beginning of August, they started the harvest of the beans and the cucumbers. Ryna would sometimes go to the farm with Pich and Kamal at dawn to pick the cucumbers when they were most cool. In the early mornings, a mist often hung over the land, and the rows of green looked like soft folds of cloth, and each cupful of air shone with its own source of pink light. When Ryna returned to the market, she always looked for Touch Pheng.

She lied to Makara and Sayon. She told them that the Khmer Rouge officer had left the village. But she could see in their eyes that they didn't believe her. "Please take this," said Sayon, and he handed Ryna the bat. It was heavy, painted half black and half red, and it had Thai writing on it. "Your husband will know what to do with this." Without replying, Ryna nodded and put the bat in the trunk that contained her clothes and her hairbrush and a few letters. She, not Sayon, would choose the time and the place of avenging her father's death.

That night, she had a dream. She and her father were in the camp, just before dawn, sitting on a log together, drinking their thin gruel of water and rice. In the distance, the dim shapes of soldiers moved about. Strangely, her father was wearing the saffron robes of a monk, but with chains cutting into the flesh of his ankles. "My dear father, what should I do?" she asked him. He touched her cheek but did not answer her question. Instead, he whispered, "Bad times." "For me?" asked Ryna. "When?" Then she was back in the dark house with Pich.

When her daughter Nita arrived at Praek Khmau on the bus, struggling with her two bags of belongings, her stomach bulging beneath her faded sarong, Ryna could hardly stop weeping with joy. "*Mi-oun, mi-oun, mi-oun,*" was all she could say. "*Mae* looks tired," said Nita, who had not seen her mother for over a year. Nita's breasts, tiny buds when she first married, had grown plump. Her lips were bright red, her fingernails and toenails the same color. "Tonight, I will make *amok* for you," said Ryna. "I will make *amok* and *luk lak* and bok choy, and I have some nice bananas. But first, you are resting." Ryna wrapped her arms around her daughter and helped her get into their oxcart. The bus stop was crowded with people and motos and carts, some of the little motos carrying entire families wedged together. One moto had a pig strapped across sideways. "Is your husband angry that you left him?" asked Ryna. "He doesn't care about me," said Nita. "I think that he has a girlfriend in Kampot. More than one." She hugged her mother.

After Nita moved in, the house was so alive and so crowded that Kamal and Pich slept in hammocks under the house, hung between the corner posts, and the oxen were retied to a stake near the kitchen shed. On the first day of Pchum Ben, they all dressed in white clothes and went to the pagoda at dawn. Several hundred villagers were already there, wearing white tops and black pants and skirts, praying and tossing rice on the ground to feed their dead ancestors. Ryna had brought along all the ancestral photographs, including the one of her father. During the Pchum Ben holidays, Ryna always thought of her parents, wondering if she might hear them as they crept about the village. But on this Pchum Ben, with the return of Touch Pheng and the flood of old memories, she was certain that she could feel her father brush past her.

"May your ancestors be released from their misery

and reborn in a happy life," chanted the three monks, who sat cross-legged on white cushions. Behind them, a long table was laden with bowls of rice and fruit, and on the wall was a large photograph of the Venerable Thy Hut, who had worked in the resettlements after the war. As Ryna sat with her eyes closed, feeling her family around her, her three daughters and her son and her husband, the thought came to her that not all of her fortune in this life had been bad. But it had not been good either. A shudder went through her as she remembered what her father had said in the dream. Was it a summary of bad things that had already happened, or a prophecy of bad things to come? Ghosts sometimes mixed future and past. Ryna half opened her eyes and saw among the throngs of people Makara and her husband, kneeling on mats. At the other side of the pagoda, beneath the photograph of the venerable monk, she saw Lakhena, sitting alone and wearing a white lace blouse with a lavender sash draped over her shoulder. Lakhena was looking intently at Ryna and her family. When she noticed Ryna looking back, she dipped her head in a bow. Ryna hesitated and then gave a slight nod in return. Lakhena surely had her own suffering, she thought, like all women. "May your ancestors bless you for what you are doing to release them from their misery and for offering them food," droned the monks.

•

A week after the dry season had begun, after the mud turned to dirt and the dirt turned to red dust that hovered like mist in the air, Ryna saw Touch Pheng limping up to her front gate. When she went down to meet him, he told her that he had come to say goodbye. He was leaving Praek Banan. It had been five months since she first saw him in the village.

"You are leaving before the rice harvest?" asked Ryna.

"I have to go," said Touch Pheng. "An old man has worn out his welcome. Do not feel sorry for me. I am alive. I'm going this afternoon, to a nephew in Banteay Meanchey. My bags are packed."

"That is a long trip on the bus."

"No matter."

The old man leaned against the gate, thin as a reed even in his traveling shirt. He would not live long, she thought to herself. "I would like my daughters to meet you before you go," said Ryna.

Touch looked at her as if he didn't understand what she had said.

"Two of my daughters are here. If you are all packed."

"I am packed," said Touch Pheng. "I do not have much." He began coughing and could not stop for a full minute. "All right," he said, taking large gulps of air. "I will meet your daughters."

With some effort, Ryna helped Touch Pheng up the ladder into her house. As always, he smelled of tobacco. He looked around without comment. Nita was napping behind the curtain, and Sreypov, just home from school, sat cross-legged in the corner with a book. Ryna introduced her daughter, who greeted the visitor and went back to her studies. The radio was playing some songs of Pen Ron. Letting his stick drop to the floor, the old man sank into one of the two chairs.

"Do you like her singing?" said Ryna.

Touch Pheng nodded. He seemed a bit out of breath and closed his eyes. Ryna was again struck by how thin he was.

"If you don't like Pen Ron, I can change the dial," said Ryna.

"Don't go to any trouble for me. Whatever you want is fine." Touch Pheng rubbed at the mole over his eye and shifted in his chair. "To be honest, Pen Ron is a little crazy for me."

"Rock and roll," said Ryna. "What about Sinn Sisamouth? There's a channel that plays Sinn Sisamouth all the time."

"I know," said Touch Pheng, opening his eyes. "I like Sinn Sisamouth. 'Violon Sneha' is my favorite song." Ryna turned the dial of the old radio until she found the Sinn Sisamouth channel. "Yes, that's him," said Touch Pheng. "It's a song I don't know, but no one can mistake his voice." He closed his eyes again.

"My husband and I listen to him all the time," said Ryna. She noticed that Touch Pheng sat so that he cocked his left ear toward the radio, as if he might be deaf in his other ear.

"No one sings like Sinn Sisamouth," said Touch Pheng. "Listen to the words. He knew the pain of romance, didn't he."

"He's my favorite singer," said Ryna. She closed her eyes, and they both sat with their eyes closed, listening to Sinn Sisamouth on the radio. Some minutes passed, how many Ryna couldn't tell. It was sweltering in the house, and she could feel the sweat dripping down the small of her back.

"Did you know that he went to medical school?" said Touch Pheng. "At one time, he was going to be a doctor. Think of that."

They could hear Nita behind the curtain. She drew long breaths as she slept, and she turned over several times.

Ryna looked at Touch Pheng. He appeared to be dozing, his head drooped down to his chest. She stood up. "What?" he said, opening his eyes and looking around as if he did not remember where he was.

"Let me give you something to eat," said Ryna.

"No need to feed me," said Touch Pheng.

"You have a long journey," said Ryna. She went down the ladder and came back with rice and pork. She watched as he ate.

"*Neang* will not eat?" he asked.

"I ate already." She served him more rice.

"Thank you," he said when he finished. "It was kind of you to allow me into your house. I doubt I will ever be back to Praek Banan." He started to rise from his chair but then sat down again. "May I ask *Neang* a favor? May I stay a few more minutes more? It is old age. I need to rest a bit after eating."

"Stay for a few minutes."

While Touch Pheng was digesting his lunch, a thought came into Ryna's head. "Why doesn't *Ta* help me make diapers for my grandchild, coming in only a few weeks."

"Diapers? I know nothing about making diapers."

"It's easy," said Ryna, "I'll show you." She got her scissors, which she had been using the night before, and a piece of cloth and cut out a square fifty centimeters on a side. Then she took out her needle and thread and began stitching around the perimeter to keep the edges from unraveling.

Touch Pheng shook his head, as if incredulous that she would ask him to do such a thing.

"It's easy," said Ryna. "We are making diapers for my first grandchild, Nita's child."

"I could never do a thing like that," said Touch Pheng.

"Of course *Ta* can. Let me just find another pair of scissors. I have plenty of cloth and thread." Ryna began looking around the room. There were not many places to look. She went through the three drawers of the table. She looked on the floor next to the car battery, where they kept a box of odds and ends. She rummaged through her trunk. Underneath her clothes, her hands felt the heavy bat that Sayon had given her, and she paused for a moment. She gripped the bat. Then she let it go. At the bottom of the trunk she found the second pair of scissors. "Here," she said, handing the old man the scissors. "Just do what I do."

"My hands," said Touch Pheng, "I have the pain in my fingers." Ryna showed him how to hold the scissors. "I cannot do this," said the old man.

"Yes, you can. Do what I do."

Touch Pheng began cutting a square out of the cloth.

"You never thought you would be making diapers, did you?"

"I have never done anything like this before," said Touch Pheng. "I have no ability at this." But he kept cutting the fabric. He was sitting forward in his chair now, concentrating. Somewhere, in the distance, the radio was still playing Sinn Sisamouth.

"Do you need any help?" asked Ryna. She pulled her chair a little closer to his.

"No, I can see what you are doing."

Even though Pchum Ben had been over for weeks, Ryna felt her father in the room. Here, now.

"*Ta* is doing a good job," said Ryna, "making diapers for my grandchild. Is it hurting your hands?"

"No, it's not hurting at all." He continued cutting. "Look, I have finished one." He held up the diaper, amazed.

They heard some rustling behind the sheet, and Nita appeared, her belly as large as a goat. "What are you doing, *Mae?*"

"Touch Pheng is making diapers for your child," said Ryna, "for my grandchild."

"That is wonderful," said Nita, smiling.

"I made a diaper," said Touch Pheng.

"Yes, you did," said Ryna, and she looked out the window just in time to see a white-breasted plover flying straight for the river.

NITA

⌒

(2009)

Limheang. Channsophea. Savada. These are the names she's considering for her daughter, still only a small bump in her belly. In another month, it will be time to announce the news. Neighbors will ride their bicycles and motos up the gravel road to the house to congratulate her and perhaps bring some cloth diapers. They'll use the visit as an excuse to inspect the rooms and the beds, to surreptitiously gawk at the refrigerator, and to see if the rumored silk curtains from Phnom Penh are really made out of silk. It's a village of farmers who can't read and dingy shop owners. It's a gossipy village. It's a village where people make sly jokes and innuendos about who is in debt and who is cheating on their spouse and who might be sneaking over the Thai border to buy and sell cocaine. Despite that small trade, the village is dirt poor, like her own village, more than three hundred kilometers away. This is her husband's family home. In her two years here, she's never been welcome. The villagers treat her politely, in deference to her rich husband.

Her face is round, with high cheeks, a strong chin, and eyebrows too inky and thick for a girl. Her teeth are good, and she has a silver star implanted on one of them, a beauty touch requested by her husband. Most of her hair has been cut short by her husband's aunt. Too short. The remaining long strands she's wrapped around her face in an imitation of the film stars she admires. Although she's only eighteen, her skin is already worn, with creases beginning to form on her forehead. But on the whole she is an attractive young woman, not what anyone would call beautiful, but pleasant-looking. Her figure is slender, like her mother's. And she has light in her eyes, an intelligence that some find appealing, and others just the opposite. At the moment, she's taking a rest and sits in the kitchen holding an ice chunk against her face to fight off the sweltering heat. She can hear her auntie retching in the next room. She misses her mother and brother and sisters. She even misses her father, who forced her to come to this place. In her mind, she composes a letter to her mother: Dear *Mae*, I'm finally pregnant. I can hardly believe it. I'd given up. Nearly three months now. Next week, I'll take the bus to Battambang City to look for baby clothes. I've learned to sew and am making something myself. A little girl is what I want. I've been a good wife, *Mae*. I have. I've kept the three flames.

She has told her mother the truth, but not all of the truth. For a moment, a slight breeze wafts through the open window, a tiny relief. She touches her tummy and thinks of the future—not her future, but the future of the little one inside her.

It was just before planting season when Pich decided that his daughter should drop out of school. They'd finished dinner, and Ryna was putting away the uneaten rice for breakfast the next morning. Nita was looking out the window; somebody's cow had gotten loose and was wandering between the houses, and the rice fields beyond the village were turning purple in the dusk. Suddenly, Pich stood up from where he'd been sitting on the floor, with no shirt on, and said, "*Kon*, I want you in the fields with me tomorrow."

"Nita has school tomorrow, and Father knows it," said Ryna.

"Other girls help their fathers in the fields," said Pich. "Sreynich, Dina, Veasna. Look at them."

"Our Nita is different," said Ryna. "She's very clever. All her teachers say so."

"Enough school," said Pich. "Thida is gone. Sreypov is too little. Kamal and I need help." He began waving his arms like he did when he was angry. Pich always looked bigger when he waved his arms. "Daughter Nita has no need of school," he said. "In a year, she's being married." Ryna let her face go slack, as she always did when she had to be a good wife and do what Pich wanted.

Nita thought to herself that she was not getting married anytime soon. Maybe when she was twenty-five. Kamal had told her that some women in Phnom Penh didn't get married until they were twenty-five or thirty and earned four hundred dollars a month all by themselves. Nita ran behind the dangling sheet where she and her little sister slept, and she put her schoolbooks inside her mother's old trunk where nobody would find them.

Early the next morning, before her father and brother got up to load the oxcart, Nita crept down the ladder and went to hide at Lina's house. It was still dark outside, so she took a kerosene lamp, but she knew the way. Lina and Nita had made many trips on the rutted road between their two houses, chatting and pretending not to notice the boys lolling under the acacia trees, doing nothing except sucking palm sugar juice out of plastic bags. "What's up, little *srey chhlat*," the boys would say to Nita. Smart cookie. Which was sweet, but maybe it wasn't really so sweet. Nita figured they just wanted her to do their math homework for them. The boys paid the teacher to get the answers to the tests, but Nita got the answers on her own. Lina, they called *sa'at*. Beautiful. They never called Nita that. Lina could have had her pick of any boy in the village, but her parents wanted her to marry her cousin Hin Nhean, so that's what she did. Then her husband left to get seasonal work in Malaysia, and the boys began looking at her again. Sometimes she looked back.

Afternoons, after their household chores, Lina and Nita walked along the river to watch the wooden fishing boats dragging their white nets behind them. Lina usually wore her knockoff Diesel T-shirt and matching flip-flops. She once offered Nita her tight-fitting Diesel—one of the boys had given it to her, and she could get many more, she said—but Nita thought it provocative. Lina had plenty of friends, but she said she liked Nita the most because Nita didn't judge her and didn't jabber all the time.

That morning, Nita hid in Lina's storage shed. She had to share the space with Lina's two cats, both strays that Lina had taken in. Nita's family had owned a cat when she was a little girl, but she had beaten it badly with a broom after she saw her father beat her mother with the broom, and the cat ran away and never came back.

All day Nita squatted in the shed, sweating in the heat. Lina brought Nita some rice and dried fish. To pass the time, they put pink polish on each other's fingernails. "I thought you'd stay in that dumb school for the rest of your life," whispered Lina. "I wish I could," Nita said. "What are your plans, sister?" said Lina. She held Nita's hand. "Why don't you live in my house with me. It's lonely when my parents go to Praek Khmau."

Live in her house with her? Lina always said a lot of silly things. She said that she'd been born to marry a rich man because she'd done a lot of good deeds in her previous life, but some crazy cosmic accident had occurred and she got stuck with her cousin Nhean. She also said that her father had seventeen girlfriends. Nita calculated that if Lina's father spent only fifty dollars on each one, it would cost more than he made in a whole year in his fish stall at the market.

Nita stayed in Lina's shed until dark, then went back to her house. Pich had been outside drinking palm wine and could barely stand up. As soon as he staggered into the house, he picked up the broom as if he was about to beat his daughter. This time he changed his mind. He just touched Nita on the shoulder and said "Daughter" and lay down on his sleeping mat.

It wasn't late, but Ryna turned off the bulb dangling from the tin roof, and the house went dark.

For a long time, Nita couldn't sleep. She was thinking about how much she would miss school and learning things, especially math, and how she would never go to university now, which had been her dream, and then she began wondering about her older sister, Thida, and if she would ever see her again, and then she was thinking about the boys who looked at Lina and wondered whether they would ever look at her that way.

The next afternoon, two teachers from Nita's school came to her house, Krou Phally and Krou Sophal. Krou Sophal was her math teacher. She had hair on her chin, like a man. Krou Phally and Krou Sophal told Nita's parents that there were only four girls left in the class, against seventeen boys, and that Nita was the best student in the entire class. In fact, the best in five years. None of the other students paid attention for one entire minute during the day. Then the teachers began complaining about how they got paid only forty dollars a month, and there was no toilet in the school. Their only satisfaction was a good student like Nita, every five years. At the least, she should be allowed to finish high school, they said. Navin "the little scientist" had finished high school three years ago and was working as a tour guide in Siem Reap and sending her parents thirty dollars a month. Two girls from the nearby town of Praek Khmau had even gone to university. Nita could be the first girl from their village to go to university. Times were changing, they said.

As the teachers were talking, Krou Sophal put her arm around Nita's shoulder—as if bonding them in a shared vision of great things for the future. A future in which Nita would graduate from high school and then go on to university like the girls of Praek Khmau and bring honor and glory to Praek Banan, and perhaps even a toilet for the school and increased salaries for its teachers. Actually, Nita had not been aware that she was the best student in five years. That knowledge solidified her ambitions. The future was beckoning.

Pich didn't say a word. He just sat picking at the dirt under his fingernails.

Nita hated working on the farm. She hated tossing the smelly cow dung and beating the rice seeds into the mud and sifting out the snails. It was stupid work. Did the other farmers think she was stupid, like them? Using her math brain to sift snails? This was temporary work, she told herself. Sometimes, she brought along a bag of salt and sprinkled it on the snails, a little at a time, and watched them slowly dissolve and turn into mush. Let them suffer a little, she thought. Suffering was part of life. At night, after she and Sreypov went behind the dangling sheet and undressed, she studied her schoolbooks with a kerosene lamp. When she was studying, she forgot who she was and where she was, and she just floated in the Land of Learning. But she knew that she would probably never be in school again.

It was a few months later that Nita's father began dropping hints about this man he knew in Battambang. Noth Bun was his name. Actually, Pich had never met this man, but his cousin in Battambang knew him. "Cousin Narith knows a rich bachelor," Pich said one night. One minute before, he'd been talking about how many kilos of rice he'd reap in the next harvest, and suddenly he was talking about Mr. Noth. A week later Pich said to Ryna, as if he was talking only to her, but loudly, "I heard that Mr. Noth is very handsome." That's all he said. Who was this Mr. Noth? Nita wondered. But she never interrupted when her parents were talking.

One afternoon, Pich said, "Mr. Noth is pretty young for somebody so rich." "How old is he?" asked Ryna. "Cousin Narith says he's thirty-eight," said Pich. "That's a good age." "How did he become rich?" asked Nita's brother, Kamal, who was allowed to interrupt. "I heard he sells rubber from the rubber trees," said Pich. "He's a businessman."

After a few weeks of this kind of talk, it was like

Noth Bun was a member of the household. Nita had never heard his name before a month ago, and now he was practically eating at their table. Of course, she knew what her father was doing. But she didn't want any of it. Look at Lina. What good did a husband do her? Nita had another friend, Chenda, who worked day and night making food for her husband and his friends and washing his clothes and his uncle's clothes and taking care of their two babies. Chenda used to be so pretty. By the time she was eighteen, her face looked like a stone. Nita's friend Sreyden had been married only six months when her husband walked out on her, leaving her with five hundred dollars of debt.

Long ago, when Nita was still a little girl, her mother had told her while they were washing clothes in the river that she didn't have to get married if she didn't want to.

Pich kept talking about this Noth Bun, and one day he announced that the man was coming all the way from Battambang to meet the family. "You should be nice to him, *kon srey*," said Pich. "It's a long trip."

"Why is he coming?" Nita asked, knowing perfectly well why he was coming.

"He wants to meet you," said Pich. "He's rich. He could take good care of you." He paused. "And maybe send a little bit to us."

"There must be other girls, in Battambang," Nita

said. She understood that she shouldn't say something with a knife blade in it to her father, but the words just came out of her mouth. Ryna looked over at Pich and waited for him to talk.

"Mr. Noth has heard that you are clever," said Pich. "And he and Cousin Narith are good friends."

"Just let him meet you," said Ryna. "You don't need to say anything to him."

Pich frowned at his wife. "Daughter should certainly *talk* to him," he said.

The next Sunday, in mid-afternoon, a big silver car drove up the rutted road to Nita's house. It couldn't get all the way, because of the mud, so it stopped about a hundred meters from the gate, and Mr. Noth began walking. It had to be Mr. Noth, thought Nita. She'd never seen a car like that in her village. She hurried down the ladder and ran to Lina's house and hid in her storage shed.

An hour later, Nita heard her mother's voice from outside the shed. "Dearest daughter, *mi-oun*, please come out now."

"I don't want to."

For a while, Ryna didn't say anything. "I know how you feel," she said.

"So don't make me come out," Nita said.

"Dear daughter . . . I love you so much. Do you understand that?"

"Yes."

"You remind me of myself when I was your age. You're prettier and smarter than I was. I was so confused. I didn't know anything about anything. I didn't really know your father. But look at us. We've made a life together. It's been twenty-five years now."

"I'm not you," said Nita.

"Your father wants you to meet Mr. Noth," said Ryna.

"What do *you* want?" said Nita.

"My dearest daughter," Ryna said in a low voice, almost whispering. She hesitated. "I want you to stay in school. But . . ." She didn't finish the sentence.

Nita sat down on an old bucket in the shed. She tossed off her flip-flops and pressed her foot hard against a rock until she could feel the pain. Nita loved her mother. She thought about how her mother was just doing what she had to do, so she came out of the shed, but she slammed the door so hard that the wood splintered, and she didn't say a word to her mother as they walked back to their house.

Mr. Noth sat in one of the two chairs of the house, Pich in the other. Pich was wearing his nice silk shirt, which he usually wore only during the Khmer New Year. Mr. Noth was dressed in a jacket and lace-up shoes. He had bushy eyebrows that met in the middle, and the hair on his head was starting to fall out, and when he stood up he leaned to one side, as if one leg were shorter than the other. Maybe it was.

Nita stood against the wall, keeping a distance. Mr. Noth knew that she'd been hiding somewhere. "I like a girl with spirit," he said, and grinned. Nita noticed that he had all of his teeth. At least he had that. Mr. Noth began asking her questions about various things, like what kinds of jobs people did in her village and the cost of tires at the market. At first, Nita didn't want to talk to him. But she knew all the answers. And she did have her dignity.

"She's a pretty girl, isn't she," said Ryna.

"Not so pretty," said Mr. Noth, "but she's clever."

"Yes, she's clever," said Pich. That was the first time in her life that Nita had ever heard her father say she was clever.

Lina was angry at Nita for planning to marry a man who lived far away. She said she'd probably never see Nita again. Battambang was on another planet, she said. But what did Lina know, thought Nita. Lina had never been outside Kandal. Neither had she. But she knew a lot of things that her mother had told her. "What will happen to me?" said Lina. "I can't go anywhere. I have no money. You'll eat good food and ride in your husband's car, and he'll take you to shops in Battambang City. How did you have such good luck?"

Nita replied that she'd rather shovel cow dung for the rest of her life than get married to Mr. Noth. Lina began shouting about how Nita didn't know about anything except her school lessons, and then Lina started in on her own rotten luck and how her husband was not making much money on the fishing boats in Malaysia. She started crying and put her arms around Nita. Lina did love her, Nita thought to herself. She told Lina things she didn't tell anyone else. She had told Lina when she had her first period.

Sreypov, too, was angry at Nita. Now she would have no sisters to play with. "Can I come with you to Battambang?" she asked. They were sitting under an acacia tree, watching some village men set up the wedding tent. Guests and distant cousins would begin arriving the next day. "You need to stay in school," said Nita. "I can go to school in Battambang," said Sreypov. "I want to come with you." "You need to stay here," said Nita. "You need to go to sixth grade, then seventh grade, then eighth grade, all the way to the twelfth grade. And then . . ." Sreypov fidgeted with a fresh scab on her knee. "Will Father let me?" she said. "Of course," said Nita. Sreypov, although only eleven, was an observant child and looked at her sister as if not believing a word. She turned and ran toward Bayon's dry good store and then on toward the fields, far from the wedding tent and her father and any prospective husbands.

The night before the last day of the wedding, Ryna had a private talk with her daughter, behind the sheet where the female children slept. Clothes hung over the sideways bamboo pole. Nita had already packed her own clothes, along with her glam photos of Pich Sophea and Sokun Nisa, which Mr. Noth said she could take with her to Battambang.

"Sweet daughter, *mi-oun*," said Ryna with tears in her eyes. "Listen to me. You have a new family now." Ryna cupped Nita's face. "It's your job to keep peace in your new family. Never complain. Always keep the three flames."

Nita had been numb during the entire wedding ceremony. She understood very well what was expected of her, and she dreaded it. "You don't have to tell me, *Mae*," she said.

"*Mi-oun*, I'm telling you again now."

"I know the three flames," said Nita. "Never take family problems outside the house. Never forget what you and Father have done for me. Always serve my husband and be respectful of him." Nita turned and looked straight at her mother, straight into her eyes. "Did you *really* want me to stay in school, *Mae*?"

"You're married now," said Ryna. She held her daughter's hand and whispered, "Don't be shy tomorrow night. You might feel uncomfortable. If you bleed, it's normal. Your husband will be happy that you're bleeding." Then Ryna gave her daughter a necklace, which her mother had given to her. It had a tear-shaped gold pendant, encircling a plant with six leaves.

Even in Mr. Noth's car, it took seven hours to drive to Battambang. Nita watched the rice fields go by, the little markets and shops on the side of the road, the motos and trucks and oxcarts plodding along.

She began living with her husband's aunt in Ang Chrum, fifty kilometers from Battambang City. Auntie's house was the house where Mr. Noth grew up. Originally, it had been a two-room wood hut on stilts, like most of the other houses in Ang Chrum, but over the years, as Mr. Noth grew more affluent, he'd built a beautiful foundation and a new roof, added rooms and modern appliances, and drilled his own water well. In the back of the house, where there had once been a toolshed, there was now a garage where Mr. Noth could park his car. A garden sprawled in the space between the house and the garage, and the entire property was punctuated with mango trees. Most of the neighbors were farmers. Their houses, shaded with acacias, were situated along little paths off the wide dirt road that served as the main street of the village. The path leading to Mr. Noth's house he had widened and paved with gravel.

It was April when Nita moved in, the hottest month of the year. Strange things happened in April. Nobody slept well. Ghosts could be heard tiptoeing about in search of water to quench their thirst. Cows broke from their tethers and went wandering through the village. Chickens magically escaped from their coops and congregated in the pagoda.

Sweating heavily, Nita unpacked her trunk and sat without moving under the fan in the kitchen. She didn't mind suffering in the heat. In fact, it seemed right that she should suffer her first months in this new place. She accepted the blame for what had happened to her, the drastic change in her future. If she'd been more clear in her wishes or spoken differently to her father or been a more loving daughter . . .

Mr. Noth stayed in the house the first two days and two nights and then drove off in his silver car. He traveled a lot and came home only a few days a month. "I want you to be happy here," he said. "Not like in that garbage dump you lived in before."

Mr. Noth also owned a second house, in Battambang City, a mansion-size house with an interior garden, cool slate floors, and countertops made of marble imported from Italy. But he told Nita that he wanted her to live with his aunt in the countryside so she would be safe.

Nita never knew what her husband did when he was gone. Once she heard him talking on his hand-phone to somebody in Chinese, and another time in Vietnamese. Auntie said she shouldn't ask.

Every time Mr. Noth came to his house in Ang Chrum, he brought Nita new clothes and beautiful shoes, like the film stars wore. "Don't wear those shoes on the road," he said. "You'll get them dirty."

"I'll wear them only with you," Nita said, and that made him smile. Mr. Noth also gave her an expensive wristwatch he'd bought in Phnom Penh. He never gave her any money. The money he gave to his aunt.

When Mr. Noth would arrive for a visit, he liked to watch Nita dress up in the new clothes, starting with the padded bras. He'd say, "You look sexy like that," and take a big drag from his cigarette. While he was looking at her, he'd limp over to the cabinet and turn on the radio, so that his aunt wouldn't hear them from her room. Then he'd take off her clothes, piece by piece. He'd take off his own clothes. He had a hairy back. It never lasted more than ten minutes, what he did to her. When he was finished, he'd kiss her and ask, "Did I hurt you?" Usually he did hurt her, but she wouldn't say anything. He didn't intention-ally hurt her, she decided. There was always a certain smell when they did it. Often, Mr. Noth had that same odor when he came home after being away. Nita figured that her husband might have girlfriends. But he'd chosen *her* for his wife. That meant a lot.

They slept together in a wide, modern bed he'd shipped from Thailand. Lying side by side with him, she could smell his shaving cream, the oil he used in his thinning hair, the alcohol and tobacco on his breath. Sometimes, she would wake in the middle of the night and feel his arm around her. Did that mean he loved her? Lina had once said that she didn't love her husband, and that he didn't love her. According to Lina, love wasn't important in a marriage. What was important, said Lina, was having a safe home with not too much fighting and a husband who wasn't drunk all the time. Nita never saw Mr. Noth drunk. And he never hit her.

Aunt Champey had red-tinted hair and very white fake teeth. To Nita, it seemed that Auntie thought of herself as about thirty years old, but she was fifty-four. She wore nice clothes, but far too tight for her plump body, and jewelry even if she wasn't going out of the house. Auntie mostly just watched TV in her room.

Auntie employed a maid named Chakrya. Auntie said to Nita, "Daughter, *kon srey*, you'll be happy. Chakrya is here to make our life easy. And we pay her plenty. Just remember that she works for me. Anything you want done, you ask me first. OK?" Nita nodded. Nita looked at Chakrya, who was the same age as her, and knew she could never ask Chakrya to do any chores for her whether Auntie gave her approval or not.

Nita asked: "What would you like me to help you with, Auntie?"

"You're my nephew's wife," said Auntie. "You don't need to do *anything* around here. You're a lucky, lucky girl." Auntie was peeling the spiny skins off some rambutans and plopping them into her mouth one after another. "You know, my nephew is a big man."

"I know," said Nita.

That night, when Nita had just come out of the shower, Auntie plunged into the bathroom without knocking and stood there looking at her naked body. Looked at her as if she were inspecting peaches at the market. Nita covered herself with a towel. Without speaking, Auntie left.

"You're a lucky, lucky girl," Auntie repeated the next day. "Not like me when I was your age. You can do whatever you want here. You hardly have to lift a finger." But there wasn't much Nita could do without any money. Whenever she asked Aunt Champey for money, Auntie said, "What do you need money for?" So during the day, Nita studied what schoolbooks she'd managed to bring from Praek Banan, sitting at a table in her bedroom, embarrassed when Chakrya would come in to clean. When she finished reading all of her books, she began reading them again. In the late afternoons, when Chakrya had to go home to help her mother, Nita cooked dinner for herself and Auntie. Auntie ate in her room, watching TV, and instructed Nita on exactly how she wanted her rice cooked and how she wanted the food put on her tray and when she wanted it delivered.

Everyone in the village took it for granted that Nita was content being married to Mr. Noth and living in the nice house. And, in some ways, she was content. Her life was easy. Certainly, she was better off than Lina or Chenda or Sreyden. But she was not living the life of her dreams. That, her father had taken away from her. When she thought of the future, she couldn't imagine living this life forever. Something must change, but she didn't know what. After a year or so, she might ask Mr. Noth if she could attend the high school in Banth Chey. That became her new dream.

One quiet night when Mr. Noth was home from his travels, after midnight, he began telling Nita the story of how his mother had died from some kind of bacterial infection. It got into her heart, the doctor said, but no one was sure. They paid a lot of money to that doctor, said Mr. Noth. He was a Vietnamese doctor and cheated them. Then Mr. Noth talked about his father and how one morning he was gone from the house, just disappeared, and never came back and never wrote one letter and never made one phone call. "I remember him so well," said Mr. Noth, closing his eyes. "I can see him this minute in my mind. I can see him clearly. He could lift me up in the air, even when I was nine years old." Mr. Noth stopped talking for a moment and looked at Nita. "I was his oldest son." Then Mr. Noth starting crying, right there with his head on Nita's lap. She stroked his cheek. "I'll be a good father," he said.

"*Bong*, don't cry," said Nita.

"Do you love me?" he said.

"Yes."

"Do you love me?" he asked again, as if he didn't believe her.

"Yes." Nita wanted to love him. Despite all that had happened and all that had been taken from her, she wanted to love him. Maybe she didn't know what love was. She stroked his cheek and watched him fall asleep.

Every night, Auntie expected Nita to rub her back for a full hour. She would be lying on the floor naked from the waist up, watching television while Nita rubbed. There was one cream to keep her back from hurting, and another cream to whiten her skin. It was hot in her room, but Auntie wouldn't let Nita open a window. She said she didn't want anybody looking at her naked.

"A lot of girls wanted to marry my nephew," she said while Nita rubbed her back. "Make clever babies for him. That's what you can do for him."

"I'm trying."

"Nephew deserves it. Look at everything that he's given us." Auntie closed her eyes and let out a contented sigh. "I used to be beautiful," she said. "Before the Pol Pot time." Then she got up and waddled over to her dresser, her bare belly drooping in great rolls over her sarong and her armpits stinking, and got out a youthful photograph of herself. "The boys. The boys . . ." She didn't finish. Then she lay down again and told Nita to get back to work massaging her.

Once, while massaging Auntie late at night, Nita blurted out that she wanted to go back to school. "What?" Auntie turned over and laughed at her, as if she'd just said that a cow had given birth to a pig. At that moment, Nita realized that she had hated Auntie from the first moment she saw her.

After Nita rubbed her back at night, Auntie would sometimes go to the corner of her room where she kept her green Buddha. While Auntie was praying, Nita clutched her mother's necklace and thought about when she might see her again. Sometimes, she imagined escaping the house at night, when Auntie was sleeping, and taking the bus home to see her mother. But it was so far, and she had no money. Other times,

Nita thought that if she went back to her village, her father would just put her to work on the farm again. Mr. Noth was not such a bad husband. He didn't beat her. He protected her. He put his arm around her when they were sleeping together. On occasion, she found herself waiting for him to come home, even waiting for him to touch her. When he called to say that he'd be home in a couple of days, she began preparing fish *amok* for him, a fancy dish he'd first eaten in a restaurant in Battambang City. He always arrived at night, and she would look out the window through the bougainvillea, searching for the tiny dots of the headlights far away, winding through the rice fields.

Mr. Noth's house in Battambang City was located in Sangkat Nary, in a neighborhood with other mansions, and there was always a guard at the front gate who greeted him with the high Sampeah reserved for royalty and monks. The guard, a kid of about seventeen, wore a uniform several sizes too large for his body and was always half asleep from the long hours. When Mr. Noth's silver car drove up, the boy would jump up to attention with his clothes bagging about, quickly sweep the pavement before Mr. Noth stepped out, and open the door. Mr. Noth acted as if he didn't even *see* the boy, but he'd leave a thousand-riel note on the

hood of the car. When Mr. Noth took Nita to Battambang City, they never stayed overnight in his big house
there. It was only for business, he said. Mr. Noth would
park his car, and then he and Nita would walk along
the wide concrete boulevard. Mr. Noth liked to go into
the shops—the stores that sold carved wood furniture,
the clothing shops pretending to import items from
abroad, the moto repair shops with boys welding and
sweating in the heat, the printing shops and the phone
shops, the tourist hotels with the white columns. The
owners all came out and shook Mr. Noth's hand. He
would joke around with his friends for a few minutes,
sharing his expensive 555 cigarettes, and then touch
Nita's shoulder and say, "This is my wife." They would
nod, but they never said a word to her.

After six months, Mr. Noth let Nita take the bus
to Battambang City by herself, once a week. It was
an hour each way, but Nita didn't mind. In the city,
she'd sit at a table in one of the restaurants owned by
Mr. Noth's friends and get a free lunch. Afterward,
she'd spend the afternoon at the Very Extraordinary
Australian University of English, a two-room house
with dirty floors and photographs of kangaroos. The
VEAUE had books in both English and Khmer. Nita
read parts of a book about Winston Churchill. She
read an accounting book. She read about the ancient
kingdom of Angkor, ten centuries ago.

After Nita's first year in Battambang, Auntie began asking her every month if she'd missed her period. Sometimes she asked her twice in the same week. "I'm not regular," said Nita. "You're not much of a wife," Auntie said. "Nephew can get any girl. Do you understand?" As Auntie was talking, she looked at Nita like she was nothing, like she was just a body for Auntie's nephew to use.

Nita called Lina and told her that she couldn't make a baby, weeping into the phone. "I've heard of girls who take two or three years," said Lina. "Don't give up." "What can I do?" said Nita. "I don't know what to do." "If the spirits want you to have a baby," said Lina, "you'll have a baby."

Another year. Two years now in Battambang. The days merged together in an unending haze. It was April again, and Nita opened every window of the house in a feeble attempt to diminish the heat. That morning, she spent a long time in the shower, almost in a daze, washing her hair and sponging off her body, and then she stood under the cool water a long while longer. Only five minutes out of the shower, she was sweating again. Auntie sprawled snoring on her bed. Nita walked into the kitchen to cook rice, but it was too hot to cook, so she went outside under a mango tree with one of her books. It was even too hot to read. She couldn't sit still, but as soon as she moved, she sweated more profusely. Mr. Noth was coming home that evening. Somehow, she managed to cook fish in the boiling kitchen. Later, that night, she looked for the headlights of her husband's car until well past midnight. Finally, she lay down on her bed with the window wide open and a single sheet over her body.

When she woke, in the dark, she felt as if she were on fire, and she was sweating through the sheet on her bed. As she slowly became further awake, she realized that she heard muffled voices outside. One voice was Mr. Noth's. There was another, a girl's voice. She got out of her bed and went to the window. It was a dark night, without a moon, but she could make out two figures. One was her husband. A moment later, Mr. Noth burst into their bedroom. "You'll have to sleep in the spare bedroom tonight," he said, hardly looking at her.

"What?" said Nita. She was still not fully awake.

"Out," said Mr. Noth. He grasped her by the arm and led her out of the room and into the spare bedroom across the hall and closed the door. What was this? Was she awake or asleep? She heard the sound of the front door opening again, and someone came in. There were other noises. "Nice." It was the voice of a girl, the voice she'd heard outside. Nita backed away from the closed door and sat down on the bed.

Could her husband possibly be bringing a girlfriend into their house? What should she do? She couldn't do nothing. This was her house. This was her husband. She went back to the closed door and listened. *"Oun,"* her husband said sweetly to the girl. Honey. The girl made some kind of sound, and then they went into the bedroom where she'd been sleeping moments ago, the room that she shared with her husband, *her* bedroom. They were laughing. There were other sounds. Rustling. Then the girl began moaning, and she heard her husband moan too. *"Oun,"* he said. Darling. The girl was saying some words too, but Nita couldn't hear what they were. Her heart was pounding. She thought to herself: Go in there right now and confront them, both of them. She couldn't let this go on, right in her own house, thrown out of her room. She imagined herself walking into the room and facing them, her cheating husband and his cheap girlfriend lying on her bed. They were both groaning now. Didn't Auntie hear all of this? Why wasn't Auntie out of her room, protesting this outrage? Nita stood at the closed door, her hands shaking. She looked out a window and saw that the moon had come out. Mr. Noth's car gleamed in the moonlight. He hadn't bothered to put it in the garage. The shadow of a mango tree draped across the hood of the car. Then she fell back on the bed and put the pillow over her head.

Sometime later in the night, she couldn't tell when, she awoke again. Screams came from the other room. Her husband was shouting, and the girl was crying. It sounded like furniture was being thrown about. The girl was screaming and screaming. Then it became quiet. Nita drifted back to sleep.

At dawn, she awoke sweating, thinking that she'd had some terrible nightmare. In her nightgown, she walked out into the hallway. The door to her bedroom was closed. The house was completely silent, except for the sound of a tree lightly brushing against the side of the house. She went to the front window, looked out, and in the dim light saw something on the gravel path in front of Mr. Noth's car. It appeared to be a body. "Oh," she shouted. She ran outside. It was a girl about twenty years old, lying in the gravel path, naked from the waist down, her buttocks and thighs bruised and scarred. The girl didn't move. Nita screamed. She ran into the house and threw open the door to her bedroom, where her husband was stretched across the bed. "A girl's on the ground outside the house," Nita shouted. "I think she's dead."

Mr. Noth sat up in bed, rubbing his eyes. "What?" he said.

"You've got to go see," shouted Nita.

Mr. Noth sleepily put on his trousers. Auntie came out of her room in her nightgown and stood in the hallway looking annoyed. Mr. Noth followed Nita out to the gravel path, where the girl was lying.

"She's dead, she's dead," wailed Nita, cupping her face in her hands and covering her eyes.

"She's not dead," said Mr. Noth. He touched the girl on her back. She didn't move.

"She's dead," screamed Nita.

Mr. Noth nudged the girl. Still she didn't move. Her eyes were closed and Nita could see that her hair was matted with blood. Mr. Noth shook the girl by the shoulder. In a few moments, she let out a moan and half opened her eyes.

"Get up," Mr. Noth said to her. Slowly, the girl lifted herself up on all fours, then to a sitting position.

"We have to take her to a doctor," said Nita. "We have to help her."

"She'll be all right," said Mr. Noth. He went into the house and came out with some clothes and put them on the ground beside the girl. He nudged the girl again. She stood up, staggered, sat down, then stood up again. Mr. Noth helped her get dressed. "Now you go home," he said to her. "I've put bus money in your pocket." The girl swayed on her feet, then slowly walked away on the gravel path out to the main road and disappeared.

That morning, Nita stood in the shower for a full half hour. She kept scraping her skin with the body brush over and over. She stayed in the shower until she heard Mr. Noth drive away in his silver car.

Mr. Noth never mentioned the incident with the girl. Neither did Auntie. A couple of times, Nita started to speak about it to Auntie, but found that she couldn't. There were no words. So all of them said nothing. And as each day passed without mention of it, the incident seemed less and less real, until it melted away like a morning mist, and Nita began wondering if it actually happened. But she moved into the spare bedroom. That small thing she did.

The next morning as Nita was serving Auntie her breakfast, Auntie grabbed her wrist. "Why aren't you sleeping in your bedroom?" Nita didn't answer. "That's your room with Nephew. You're a silly girl. When Nephew comes home next month, I want you back in that room with him. Do you understand?"

"I'm not going back," said Nita.

"Yes, you are," shouted Auntie, and she gave Nita's wrist a rough twist.

"I'm not," said Nita. She pulled herself away from Auntie's grip.

A week after she'd moved into the spare bedroom, Nita missed her period. She missed again the next month. She felt nauseated.

"You're pregnant," said Auntie, and she hugged Nita. "Am I pregnant?" Nita asked, disbelieving. "I'm sure of it," said Auntie. She gently placed her hand on Nita's stomach. "You're pregnant, my dear." Nita looked at herself in the mirror. "You're pregnant," Auntie said again and laughed. "After all of this time. I've been saying prayers for Nephew. You took a long time."

When Mr. Noth came home a few weeks later, he put his hand on Nita's stomach and smiled. "Our son," he said. After a day's visit, he drove back to Battambang City.

"His business with the rubber," said Auntie.

"He can stay away as long as he wants," said Nita. Just the day before, she'd finished moving the rest of her clothes into the spare bedroom.

"You'll have a clever baby boy," said Auntie. "Maybe we should name him Chamness."

Nita thought to herself that she could possibly have a son. Her husband and aunt wanted a son, but Nita decided that she was going to have a daughter. In fact, a daughter would be better. She began to be more careful about what she ate. In the mornings, she walked to the market and picked out the fruits and the vegetables. Pork, which had always been a favorite, she stopped eating because she heard that the local pigs had been contaminated with dirty water. She began taking naps in the afternoon. She took up sewing, to make clothes for the baby. On one of her trips into Battambang City, she got a sewing book and needles and yarn with a tiny bit of money Auntie had given her, and she taught herself to sew. Some mornings, she sat in a rocking chair in her new bedroom near the open window and began sewing a tiny shirt for her daughter. With the light streaming in, it was quiet, and peaceful. It was a small room, but it had everything she needed. As she sat sewing, Nita began concentrating on small things. She looked carefully at the way tiny specks of dust in the air danced in the sunlight and the way that the feathery boundary between shadow and light slowly moved across the floor as the hours passed. She studied her own hands, hands that would hold her daughter, and noticed how the lines on her palms crisscrossed in mysterious patterns and how the blue veins just beneath the skin of her wrists slightly bulged. In the early mornings, she inhaled the scents of mangoes and newly lit fires and damp earth that wandered through the house. She listened to the sounds of the farmers yoking their oxen and chickens pecking and women gathering wood.

Auntie had stopped mentioning Nita's move into the spare bedroom. There were other things to complain about. In fact, Auntie hadn't been feeling well lately. She seemed tired and began going to bed right after supper. A few days later, she complained about dizziness and headaches. But Auntie had always complained about something. Then she began retching. This went on for a week, until she couldn't get out of bed in the morning. "Call my nephew," she moaned from her bed. When Mr. Noth arrived two days later, he picked Auntie up in his arms and drove her to a hospital in Battambang City.

Auntie was given various medicines and sent home. But the nausea and fatigue persisted. Mr. Noth came back and sent her to different specialists. Each diagnosed an illness in his specialty and prescribed more medicines, but Auntie didn't get any better. Mr. Noth wanted to take her to Thailand or Vietnam for another diagnosis, but Auntie refused. So she remained in a weakened state, barely able to get out of bed, nauseated and dizzy. Nita knew what was wrong with Auntie. Nita was putting a small amount of pesticide in her food every day. She'd read a book about agriculture in the Very Extraordinary Australian University of English, and she had computed exactly what dose to use, making Auntie sick but not ill enough to die. For breakfast, lunch, and dinner, she brought the food into Auntie's room. At other times of the day, when Nita heard Auntie calling out for water or for help going to the toilet, she sometimes didn't answer the call. Nita was in control now. In another few months, she would leave Battambang altogether, she'd decided. She would take the bus while her husband was away, using money she'd taken from Auntie's drawer. She would go back to her village in Kandal and give birth to her daughter surrounded by her family. And there she would stay. It had all been temporary—the work on the farm, the marriage, the move to Battambang.

At night, as she lay on her bed, Nita imagined that she could see her daughter curled up inside her. Her daughter was a perfect being. She'd made the little thing herself from her own body. A feeling like warm water moved through her insides where her daughter slept. She would be a good mother, she was certain, like *Mae*. She would nurse her daughter and bathe her and watch her grow. Her daughter would be clever, and she would go to university. And Nita would always be her mother. Thinking these nice things, she slipped into sleep. She dreamed that she was a queen standing in a great house, grander than Mr. Noth's house in Battambang City. When she looked out, the glassy stone floors went on and on until they joined with a garden. Beautiful spirits hovered in the air all around her, blessing her and her daughter. And there was beautiful music from invisible instruments. *Mae* was there, and Father was there. Sreypov and Kamal were there. And dear Thida, smiling at her. And Lina. Everyone was so kind. And milk poured from her body, white and perfect and good.

KAMAL

◯

(2013)

Old Hok died in his little room next to the pagoda. The day after the cremation, at dawn, Kamal went to gather up the monk's few things. Months before, the old man had willed him his sparse property.

In the early morning, the village was quiet, except at the hour when the monks walked in procession to the river to bathe. An oxcart stood near the pagoda, shadowy in the dim light. As Kamal ambled down the dirt road, thinking of old Hok, his feet made little clouds of red dust. It was the dry season. When the rains came, the road filled with puddles and mud.

Old Hok had been sick for two years, during which he hardly rose from his sleeping mat, and the air in his room was hot and stale and smelled like an old man.

Kamal had never before been in Hok's room. On the one shelf, Kamal found musty copies of *The Unfaithful Woman* and *King Mongkut*, an ink-stained envelope of photos, and a pair of spectacles with glass as thick as the bottom of a beer bottle. He paused a moment to flip through the photos: one showed Hok as a young man, standing in front of a grand palace somewhere. Another showed the monk on a beach with mountains rising in the distance. Another, a crowded city. Closing the envelope, Kamal felt a stab of bitterness that his work on the farm had never allowed him to see the world. He gingerly put the shelf's items in his burlap bag, as well as the small statue of the Buddha and the photograph of the Venerable Thy Hut. There were no clothes aside from the monk's sandals and saffron robes. Behind the room, amid the wilted garden, Hok's broken bicycle leaned against an acacia tree. Kamal had known the old man for most of his life. It was believed that Hok might be a third or fourth cousin. However, Kamal's parents never spoke about Hok. Years ago, there had been some argument, which no one could remember now, and Pich had forbidden any mention of the monk thereafter. Kamal couldn't imagine old Hok ever arguing with anyone.

Since the last harvest, Kamal and Pich had been spending their days threshing the rice sheaves against a wooden board in back of their house, catching the grains of rice in a large yellow sheet and then shoveling the rice into burlap bags. It was a mind-numbing task, but easier than tending the fields, and Kamal liked to listen to his mother singing her songs as she sewed. The men started threshing at dawn and worked until dusk, when the houses began to glow softly with their kerosene lamps, and the smells of cooked chicken and ginger wafted through the village.

After Kamal finished eating dinner with his parents and sisters, he and his friends usually met in the rutted main road, then walked past the vegetable gardens and nervous cows until they reached the dry goods store opposite the market. There, the young men reclined in the white plastic chairs and drank palm wine until the surrounding fields disappeared into the night. Many of Kamal's childhood friends had moved away from Praek Banan to get work. Of those remaining, many were married, and some even had children, but they'd been meeting together for years, and domestic affairs could always be forgotten for a few hours.

"Any of you guys want old Hok's bicycle?" Kamal said, and he took a deep swig of palm wine from a recycled laundry detergent container.

"Why would anyone want that piece of shit," said Narin, a tall boy who was trying to grow a beard.

"It can be fixed," said Kamal. He waited to see if

there was any interest. Most of the young men owned motos and disdained bicycles. "I'll keep it if nobody wants it." The boys grunted and continued playing cards without comment. Hok and his bicycle meant nothing to them, thought Kamal. He'd keep the bicycle himself, but he'd have to hide it from his father.

Across the road, a kerosene lamp came to life in Bormey's house. Chivon dropped his cards and stared intently across at the house. Many times, Chivon had wanted to walk alone with Bormey by the river, but custom and her parents forbade it, unless they became engaged. Nevertheless, he and Bormey were in love, or so they told people. Kamal had never been in love, although he had kissed Narin's sister a few times.

"Old Hok was bad luck," said Narin. "One of our chickens dropped dead every time he came to visit."

"You can't blame that on old Hok," said Kamal. "Your scrawny-ass chickens were dying because you didn't feed them." Kamal was drunk. He was thinking about what an adventurous life Hok had led, despite being a monk, and how everyone in the village thought he was just a tiresome old man who didn't know anything. Kamal had shared many meals with Hok when the old monk was up on his feet. Many stories he'd heard from old Hok about his travels in Laos and Thailand and Australia, the foods people ate, the ships in the harbors, the buckets of money just lying in the road. According to Hok, in Australia he'd met a woman who wanted to marry him, and he'd come a whisker's breadth from renouncing the monkhood and running off with her. With a laugh, he'd given Kamal a crumpled map of Australia and a knife with a beautiful carving of a dog on its handle. Now Hok was gone. Nobody knew of his exciting life except for Kamal and Hok's other friend, crazy man Sok Rith. Kamal held one of his cards in the candle and watched it catch fire and shrivel into a black crisp.

The week after Hok's passing, the village began preparing for the Khmer New Year, and Chhay's cousin Sophea arrived for her annual visit.

She stayed with her uncle and aunt. Kamal followed a distance behind her as she walked to the market in her high heels. He waited in the stall that sold mangoes and rambutan, then followed her back to her uncle's house. Her long silky hair swayed as she moved. Even under the shade of the covered stalls, her skin was so light she could pass for a *barang*. Her stylish and low-cut blouses, most likely bought in the shops of Phnom Penh, revealed the curves of her breasts. Some of the merchants would shoo her away as she approached their stalls. But Chhay, who sold fried crickets and grasshoppers, always welcomed her into his stall and offered her a warm can of Coca-Cola. Sometimes, Sophea met her childhood girlfriends at the market, and they locked arms like schoolgirls and spent a half hour chatting under the awning of the fabric shop.

Following the evening hours with his friends, Kamal walked by her uncle's house, hoping to get a glimpse of her through the open window. When he couldn't see her inside, he sat in the dark next to the chicken coop and found himself mumbling Buddhist prayers, something he never did even at the pagoda. He saw her smooth skin when he went to sleep that night and, the next day, heard her voice in the sounds of the boys' kites, whose arched bamboo struts and wrapping paper hummed in the wind.

After a game of Chol Chhoung one evening in mid-week, Kamal overheard two men talking, both drunk and smoking cigarettes.

"The little whore is back," said one of the men.

"A pricey whore."

"Did you see how she was looking at Tararith today at the market?"

"How was that, brother?"

"Straight in the eye. And long. Rith's wife chased her away."

"She's a slut, all right. She's looked at me just like that."

"You couldn't afford her."

The men began laughing, showing their tobacco-stained teeth in the light of their lantern. Kamal should have walloped them, he later told himself. He was twenty-seven years old and far stronger, but instead he only slammed his fists together and walked home on the dirt road.

That night, lying on his mat next to the oxen, Kamal couldn't sleep. His father was snoring beside him, and above, in the house, he could hear his sister Nita singing to her baby. It was a happy song. Nita had settled quickly back into the family after leaving her husband. Only a month earlier, Mr. Noth had arrived at their house in his big silver car, having driven all the way from Battambang, and demanded that Nita and her baby be returned to him. However, as soon as he saw that the child was a little girl, he departed empty-handed.

There were other night sounds as well. Mr. Noeum and his wife were shouting at each other as usual. Across the way, their neighbor Mr. Em was rambling around his two rooms, laying out sweet sticky rice to feed the ghost in his house. Cousin Nimol had once seen that particular ghost and swore it was Mr. Em's deceased aunt Menghun, but Mr. Em vociferously denied it. He wouldn't be caught dead giving anything to Aunt Menghun, he said, and certainly not sweet sticky rice.

Kamal put his hands over his ears and tried to sleep. He often found himself occupied with Sophea during her visits home, but something felt different this time. Perhaps the ugly comments made by the two drunks had disturbed him more than he'd realized. This visit, Sophea somehow seemed more glamorous, more mysterious. He'd heard her speaking on her handphone in English, and in Thai. He remembered how he used to see her as a little girl helping her mother make cakes for the monks. He remembered her washing clothes in the river. When she got older, he sometimes talked to her in the market or at birth ceremonies. By age eighteen, she was the most beautiful girl in Praek Banan and miraculously still unmarried. Then she had suddenly disappeared. It was rumored that she'd gone to Phnom Penh to earn money to pay back a family debt. There were other rumors. Some people said that she lived in a guesthouse in Bangkok. Others said that she was the mistress of a wealthy Korean businessman. A year went by. Then another. Her parents accepted the fat envelopes of money she sent them each month, but they would not allow her to set foot in their house again. In the second year she was gone, her uncle Sovann offered her a place in his house near the pagoda. But Sophea came back to the village only for occasional visits. Each time, she brought gifts. Beautiful shoes for the girls. Bottles of French wine that people studied and put on their shelves but never dared open. Fragile crystal glasses that looked like they might shatter if anyone sneezed. After a week's visit, Sophea would drive away in her white Land Rover.

As Kamal lay on his sleeping mat thinking of Sophea, a warmth spread through him like palm wine. Why had he never tried to contact her after she'd left the village? Why had he never talked to her on her visits home? And suddenly he knew that all of these years he'd been waiting to marry her.

The next evening, after dinner, Kamal spoke to his parents about the girl. It was mid-April and ninety degrees even at night. Drenched in sweat, Kamal held a wet cloth to his face as he talked. His father sprawled at the wood table, shirtless as usual, attempting to tally up the meager number of fifty-kilo bags of rice they'd filled the past week. Pich had no facility for math, but he knew the harvest this year wasn't good. He slammed down his pencil when he grasped the meaning of his son's faltering words.

"Are you my son? Are you crazy? That girl is nothing but a fancy *srey bar*. She's a whore." Pich stood up and began pacing the small room. Although a short man, his head struck the one light bulb dangling on a wire from the ceiling, and shadows swung back and forth across the room.

"Please, Husband," said Ryna. *"Ouv Wea* should

take care what he says." Ryna put aside her sewing needles and glanced anxiously at her youngest daughter, Sreypov, who was cleaning the dishes with a scrub brush and a tin can of water.

"Take care?" shouted Pich. "It should be Kamal who takes care, Kamal more dumb than a cow."

At the sound of her father's booming voice, Nita, who had been nursing her baby girl, appeared from behind the dangling sheet that partitioned off the women's area of the house. Thida ceased massaging her mother's back.

"That girl has been the whore of rich men," said Pich. "More than one."

"She has a sweet heart," said Ryna. "Look how she's helped her family. They would have lost everything. What would have happened to Botum and Bunrouen? And Kanya and Devi and little Seyha?"

"Are you crazy too?" hollered Pich. "Do you want our son marrying a whore?" Thida stood up and went behind the women's sheet.

"You probably also think you're going to move to Phnom Penh," Pich said to Kamal. "Live with that whore in the big city."

Kamal looked over at his mother. For a short while, it appeared that she would challenge her husband, as she occasionally did, but she only sighed and began smoothing out the shirt she'd just made for the

Khmer New Year festivities. She turned to Kamal, sitting on the floor next to the car battery. "Dear son, there are many girls you can marry. Lina and Rany's daughter. Dara's daughter. Nary and Falla's daughter. You're good with your hands. You're handsome. And I'm not the only one saying that." Kamal's mother had said exactly the same thing many times in the last few years, changing only the names of the available young women. He knew that she loved him, but she didn't know his heart.

While his mother was suggesting brides, Kamal pictured in his mind how Sophea had looked that morning at the market as she placed various items in her basket. Her hands were as delicate and smooth as the hands of an apsara dancer, not like the hands of the other girls in the village. And he remembered the proud way that she carried herself, undaunted by village gossip. He had almost gone to speak to her then. Surely she must have noticed his stare, but she had just flipped her hair to one side and walked on to the next stall to purchase some fresh river fish. Around her left ankle was a thin silver chain with several turquoise stones. Kamal was willing to admit that Sophea might be getting her money by sleeping with one or two rich men in Phnom Penh. But hadn't she done so to help her family, as his mother said? Was that wrong? She'd kept her dignity. Kamal could see that. He knew unmarried girls here in Praek Banan who would tell any lie to get what they wanted. And some of them weren't virgins either. Sophea was dignified and honest, and she had wanted to know the world. What was the sinfulness in that?

"I don't need to hear any more about this whore," said Pich. He sat down heavily on the bamboo floor across from Kamal. For a moment, Kamal feared that his father would strike him. "It looks like we might have only twenty or twenty-five extra bags of rice this year," said Pich. "Half what we had last harvest. We'll sell them to Duy when he comes around in his truck."

Kamal nodded. Somehow he must talk to her, he thought to himself, tell her of his admiration and intentions. But how? And then what? He tried to imagine the future, but he could not get past this moment, with the sound of his father's voice in his ears.

"Duy will cheat us like he did last year," said Pich. "Then he'll sell our rice to his friends in Vietnam for a nice profit. But what can you do." Pich stood up. "I'm sleeping." He picked at the dirt under his fingernails. Then he climbed barefoot down the rickety wood ladder and lay on his sleeping mat in the storage area below the house. Disturbed, the chickens squawked and scattered in all directions. Kamal looked down between the bamboo poles of the floor and watched as his father performed his nightly ritual of wrapping his checkered *krama* twice around his neck for good luck. Nearby, in the slatted light, was his own mat, their motos, and their two oxen tied to a wood post. He and his father had been sleeping below ever since Nita escaped Mr. Noth and moved back with the family. Kamal figured there was one benefit to the new sleeping arrangement. Pich didn't have to call out to Ryna for help getting up the ladder when he returned home drunk in the middle of the night, waking up the neighbors and embarrassing the family. Long ago, Kamal had vowed that he would never be like his father. Yet here he was, a farmer, working on his father's farm, sleeping next to his father on their straw mats. He looked at his hands, the hands of a farmer. For now.

"Brother, don't feel sad," whispered Thida. She had come back into the room and sat beside Kamal. "You'll find a wife. Rany is rich. And his daughter is not so bad to look at." Kamal was staring at the muffled shadow cast by the hanging bulb and was turning a kernel of corn over and over in the palm of his hand. "What are you thinking, dear brother?" said Thida. She was the daughter closest in age to Kamal, the daughter who helped her mother with the cooking and cleaning while Sreypov studied her school lessons and Nita took care of her baby. Thida was also the daughter who knew most about the affairs between women and men. "You're thinking of Sophea, aren't you, dear brother."

Kamal nodded. "I can't bear it," he whispered.

"I'll take a letter to her for you," said Thida.

Kamal rose and held his sister's hand. He hesitated, overwhelmed by her offer. "I am being grateful to you for the rest of my life," he said. "Father will change his mind. I think he will. He's worried now about the bad harvest. I'll speak more strongly to him next week. If he can just meet Sophea, if he can talk to her . . ."

A sequence of possible events began forming in Kamal's head. Sophea would receive his letter, and she would understand his feelings for her, and also his worthiness. He would show her that he was a modern man, who knew about more than just farming. He'd learned to use the Internet in Praek Khamu. He could talk to her about palaces in Thailand and the plains of Australia. Pich would eventually give his approval after he understood that Sophea was not what he thought. After getting married, Kamal and Sophea would travel together. He wanted to see Phnom Penh again, and Sihanoukville, and even Bangkok. Surely, Sophea had been to Bangkok. What a strange and wonderful place it must be. She would show him Bangkok. And then, perhaps, they would open a shop in Phnom Penh. Clothing? Printing? It hardly mattered. Undoubtedly, Sophea would want to stay in Phnom

Penh. They would live in Phnom Penh. Phnom Penh! Although only ninety kilometers, the place seemed as far away as the moon. Kamal thought of the one time he'd been to Phnom Penh, five years ago, to visit an uncle who needed help in his print shop. The city was even more awesome than the stories Kamal had heard, with wide paved streets and blinking lights and hundreds of cars and tall buildings made of metal and glass and shops and stores one after the other and people crowding the streets as thick as new shoots of grass. And the constant explosion of buzzing and honking, and the grinding of thousands of invisible machines. Uncle had introduced Kamal to his friends. They worked in banks and computer stores. Mr. An was employed in the Ministry of Mines and Energy and wore a suit and tie. "Shake their hands but don't say anything," Uncle advised. The first day, Uncle had shown Kamal how to use a toilet. It was in the back of his shop. Kamal worked for his uncle for a month and learned how to take orders and write up receipts. Each night, he slept with Uncle's grandson in a bed, a soft cushion high off the floor. He remembered exactly what the street looked like from the window of Uncle's house, the tiny market on the corner with the blue awning and the lady sitting on a white stool selling fried pork. How often he could see that little market in his mind.

The thought of Phnom Penh now filled Kamal with excitement, and dread. He looked at his hands again and saw the hands of a farmer. But that was the past. Sophea would show him the secrets of Phnom Penh. She would introduce him to interesting people, as his uncle had done. Kamal imagined himself an explorer, like Marco Polo, or like old Hok. But . . . how could he take care of his parents and sisters if he lived in Phnom Penh? Perhaps his father should sell the farm. Might he do it? The farm had been in the family for at least four generations. According to family legend, Pich's grandfather had received the farm in a shadowy deal with a corrupt French official during the 1920s, but the farm may have been in the family even longer than that. All the family records had been lost during the Pol Pot time. Yes, they should sell the farm, Kamal decided. He could also send money home.

With this flood of ideas and plans going through his head, Kamal climbed down the ladder and got on his sleeping mat without removing his clothes. As he lay there looking out toward the road, the posts of the front gate shone like white cloth in the light of the moon. That night Kamal dreamed that he and Sophea were in a boat drifting down the river. She reclined with her head in his lap, and her silky hair wrapped his waist like sweet loving arms.

Sophea did not respond to his letter. Kamal sent a second letter, which his sister placed in the girl's hand as she walked out of the pagoda one day. She didn't reply to that one either.

At Thida's advice, Kamal asked Ming Oeun, the matchmaker, to speak to Sophea's parents. Oeun was a talkative woman, the wife of the village chief, with a good stock of magic beads she employed for her missions. However, she had scarcely begun her long speech when Sophea's parents announced that the girl was no longer their daughter. Talk to the uncle, they said. The matchmaker then went to Sovann's house near the pagoda. It was mid-morning, the best time of day for such business. "With gracious respect, and all due courtesy, I am coming to your door on behalf of Kamal," said Ming Oeun, and she vigorously rubbed the beads hidden in her hand. "I understand," said the uncle. Sovann would have been a handsome man had he not been missing most of his teeth. When he spoke, his voice made a whistling sound as the air forced its way through his fractured mouth. "But I'm afraid that I cannot make decisions for my niece. Do you know the girl? She has her own mind."

Ming Oeun relayed the news to Kamal and returned the riel notes he had advanced her for the job. "Dear boy, you will have to make your intentions known directly to her." Then Ming Oeun paused.

"After all, she's already twenty-three years old and knows the world." Although Oeun was a kindhearted woman, who had happily facilitated a great many matches, Kamal heard in her voice a note of reproach, perhaps a sly comment on the manner in which Sophea had amassed her great wealth.

On the last day of the Khmer New Year observance, Kamal spotted Sophea standing alone beneath a banyan tree. She wore a blue silk dress with a white silk blouse and a gold-colored collar around her neck, and her hair was folded in a bun held together by a wreath of white flowers. With her head gently tilted to one side, as if listening to the monks, she seemed to be in a world of her own even though all her relatives were only meters away, kneeling in the pagoda. And there was a sadness about her that Kamal had never seen before but that burrowed itself deeply into his soul, and the sadness and the perfume in the air made him feel like he were floating far beyond the village. He had to talk to her, now. She would be returning to Phnom Penh in the morning.

Stiff in his ceremonial clothes and perspiring in the heat, he walked toward her. She looked up, and a strand of her hair came loose and fell upon the white curve of her neck.

"*Bong* Kamal," she said. As soon as she spoke, he realized that he had no notion of what he would say to her. She asked him if he was enjoying the celebration. He said something in reply. She remarked that she had offered a prayer for her parents even though they wouldn't speak to her, and also a prayer for her deceased grandfathers and grandmothers. While she talked, she turned a silver bracelet around and around on her wrist.

"Sophea, did you get my letters?"

She smiled. "How many were there?"

"Two. There were two."

She gave a small laugh and tossed her head, and another strand of hair slipped from its flower clasp and dropped to her shoulder. At that moment, her uncle and aunt and cousins came out of the pagoda with plates of *kralan* cakes, and she joined them under a white canopy. Kamal stood for a while next to the banyan tree, his thoughts a confusion of odd angles. Then he joined his own family in the pagoda.

That night, Thida whispered to him, "Maybe she's not the right girl for you, dear brother."

"Please do not say such things," said Kamal. They were in the toolshed, and he was sharpening the blade of the plow. Planting season was one month away. "I have not shown her my heart, and my strength." Despite his failures so far, he was more determined than ever. He would prove his worthiness. For starters, he would begin going to the pagoda every morning at dawn, before he and his father went with their oxcart to the fields. If any spirits were about, they would see his devotion and come to his aid.

In mid-May, planting began. Kamal and Pich started with rice. In the coming weeks, they planted kasava, corn, and cucumbers. When the rice seedlings were twenty centimeters tall, an intense yellow velvety green, it was time for transplanting. Transplanting was always tedious work and murderous on a farmer's back, even for Kamal. They had to stoop down and lean over, dig their trowels into the mud, and scoop up the young rice plants one by one, careful not to damage the roots. Then carry the plants to the new field and bury them in the mud. After two days, Kamal's back hurt so much that he couldn't sleep at night, but the work went on for a week. His father had his own solution for the pain. He drank palm wine every night until he was beyond drunk. Even then, Pich moaned during the night, sat up on his mat every hour, walked around, and lay down again in a stupor.

In the fields, Kamal and Pich worked side by side in silence. A number of times, Kamal wanted to talk to his father about Sophea and the life he imagined with her, but he couldn't think of the right words to say. Pich had never been much of a talker himself. On the fifth day of transplanting, after a lunch of rice and bits of pork, Kamal was digging up a plant when he heard a scream. He looked up to see his father writhing on the ground. "Father," he shouted. Pich groaned. His eyes were closed. "Are you all right?" Kamal said. He kneeled down over his father and touched his arm. Pich waved him away. He tried to stand up, then crumpled to the ground again. "Father." "I'm all right," said Pich. Kamal kneeled down again and held his father's hand. "Twisted ankle," said Pich. He tried to stand up again but couldn't. "You shouldn't work any more today," said Kamal. "I need to work," said Pich. "You need to rest," said Kamal. Kamal bent over and picked up his father in his arms and carried him to the oxcart. He was surprised at how light his father was, like one bag of rice.

Kamal did not have to wait a whole year to see Sophea again. She came back to the village in August for the wedding of her good friend Srun Kimleang. Kimleang was the last of her childhood friends to get married. Kamal waited to talk to Sophea outside her uncle's house, but she had already sequestered herself with the bride to prepare the many dresses and hairpieces Kimleang would wear.

On the second day of the wedding, Kamal and

his family and Sophea and her uncle and aunt joined the other villagers in the groom's procession to Kimleang's house, while the musicians marched behind and family friends carried pigs' heads and plucked chickens for the evening's feast. In the wedding tent, Kamal sat only three rows from Sophea. Although a bridesmaid, she spoke to no one around her, and Kamal sensed again that terrible aloneness he had witnessed before, which did not subside even through the joke telling and the ritual hair cutting of the bride and groom.

The old *ta acha*, who had already performed two marriages in Praek Banan that month, stood in front of the young couple and turned to Kimleang. "Be respectful to your husband, serve him well, and keep the three flames." Kimleang nodded. The bride and groom exchanged rings.

When the parents tied the red string around the wrists of the bride and the groom, Sophea began quietly weeping. Kamal burned to take her into his arms.

That evening, after the wedding dinner, Kamal managed to sit at the same table as Sophea. Her melancholy of earlier in the day had vanished, and she talked with her friends and accepted numerous invitations to dance. He noticed how the men looked at her, even some of his own friends, and she smiled at each of her partners, although none of them were worthy of her in Kamal's view. As she spun and turned to the music, her hair gleamed in the rented fluorescent lights and flowed like the morning river.

Finally the moment arrived when Kamal was alone with her. "I am happy to see you again," he said, gripping his leg fiercely to give himself courage.

"Thank you," she said.

He handed her a new letter. She read it without comment. He studied her face. What was she thinking? Another dance started, and a song blared from the speakers on the canopy posts. The music was so loud he could see the lemonade vibrating in her cup. Somewhere, people were singing an old harvesting song. What was she thinking?

He looked at her, and she was perfect. She was the world. She put her arm on the table. Her hand lightly brushed against his hand. "You are sweet, Kamal," she said to him. "If you want to talk to me, come to my house in Phnom Penh." She took a piece of paper from her purse and wrote down her address. She mentioned a date a month away.

Kamal felt his blood pounding in his ears. The music crashed and crashed. "I will do it," he heard himself say.

"Do you know Phnom Penh?" she said.

"I will get there. You can be sure of that."

"I live near Wat Langka. All the tuk tuk drivers

know where that is. Go to Wat Langka and ask for directions to my street."

Kamal nodded and mumbled something. Suddenly, he felt that he should leave the tent before Sophea changed her mind. He said goodbye and hurried away.

The next two weeks went by in a blur. Kamal began brooding over what clothes he would wear to Phnom Penh. He owned nothing suitable. Day after day, as he and his father began harvesting the cucumbers, he thought about this problem. The rainy season had started, creating a lavender mist that hung over the river. On the other side of the fields, the palm trees huddled together on their long skinny trunks like a bunch of girls gabbing at the market.

"Do you have a nice shirt you can lend me?" he asked Chhay one Sunday when he was eating lunch at his friend's house. He had known Chhay since primary school and trusted him above all of his friends.

"You must be joking," Chhay said, and made one of his monkey grins.

"He had a nice shirt when I married him," said Kunthea, Chhay's wife. "I haven't seen it for three years." Chhay's little boy climbed up onto Kamal's lap.

"Then can you lend me some money?" said Kamal. "I'll buy a shirt in Praek Khmau." He reached down and tickled the child's feet.

"Of course, brother," said Chhay. "And I'll take one hundred percent of the credit when you achieve victory. It would be a relief for Cousin Sophea to get married."

"You don't need a nice shirt," said Kunthea. "From what I hear, most of the girls are already in love with you."

"I don't believe that," said Kamal. "And even if it were true, I don't want most of the girls."

Kunthea wagged her head at Kamal as if he were a spoiled child. "Sophea must already love you. She invited you to Phnom Penh. She's never invited us to Phnom Penh."

"We can go to Phnom Penh on our own," said Chhay. "We went just a year ago."

"Do you know Phnom Penh?" Kunthea asked Kamal. "Did Sophea tell you how to find—"

"Of course I know Phnom Penh," Kamal said. He abruptly pushed his chair back and stood up, spilling his cup of tea. "Do you think I've never been to Phnom Penh?" he shouted. Immediately, his hand flew up to cover his mouth. Chhay and Kunthea were both staring at him in shock. Kamal looked at Chhay and then at Kunthea. "I'm . . . I'm so sorry," said Kamal. "I'm so sorry."

"You must be nervous about this whole thing," said Chhay.

"Everything will be OK," said Kunthea, avoiding Kamal's eyes. She began clearing the plates from the table.

On the day that Kamal started his trip to Phnom Penh, the heat was not diluted by the rains, and he was already sweating when he got on his moto to follow the road to Praek Khmau. There, he would catch the three o'clock bus to the city. Passing the flooded rice fields and oxen and occasional cluster of tin-roofed houses along the road, he rehearsed the words he planned to say to Sophea. At two o'clock, he arrived in Praek Khmau. After locking his moto to a metal post, he took a seat on a crumbling wooden bench in the bus station. In his hand, he held the piece of paper she had given him with her address. Occasionally, he glanced at the painfully slow clock on the wall. An hour passed. The bus did not come. His new shirt was wet against his skin. Another hour passed. Then another. At ten minutes past five, the bus arrived with no apologies. With an anxious sigh, Kamal sat down near the front so that he could be first off. Only a few other people occupied seats on the bus—an elderly couple who would not stop chattering about meeting their son, and a single man who stared out the window. At Chrey Thum, a Muslim family boarded the bus and went straight to the back. A handful of others got on at Praek Sdei and then at Praek Ambel and Roka Khpos, and the farms went by one after another in the early evening light. The road widened. Kamal began to see cars and low buildings and crowds of people on the street as they approached the outskirts of Phnom Penh.

By the time the bus came to a stop at the Central Market in Phnom Penh, at half past seven, it was dark. He was already two hours late for his appointed visit with Sophea. Next to the bus station loomed a vast mountain of a building, several stories high, lit up as if several fires blazed within it. In the distance, he could see silhouettes of other buildings. Throngs of people and cars and motos buzzed and throbbed through the streets even though many of the shops had closed for the night. Kamal got off the bus, confused.

He had not been in this area of Phnom Penh during his visit five years ago.

In front of him, lights on a shop sign flashed on and off: "Angkor Samnang" "Angkor Samnang" "Angkor Samnang." He stepped on a bottle and heard the crunch of the glass. Looking down, he saw that the street was littered with bottles and paper. After a car nearly hit him, he hurried onto a side road.

Remembering the purpose of his trip, he walked toward a group of tuk tuks parked outside a restaurant.

A man and woman, well dressed, stood by the entrance and smoked cigarettes. They looked at him casually, as if he were a leaf blowing by in the wind, and continued their conversation.

"I wish you had brought me somewhere else."

"I thought you liked this place."

"I never said I liked this place."

"Yes, you did."

Kamal spoke to one of the tuk tuk drivers, who said he knew Wat Langka. It was near Independence Monument. They drove past shops crammed together side by side and on top of each other. Farther, gates of houses, small groups of men playing cards, starved-looking dogs. At Wat Langka, Kamal got out of the tuk tuk and paid for the trip. He asked about Street 308. The driver waved vaguely in a southerly direction. Now the streets were shadows, lit only by the occasional light in a house. Kamal set out on foot, walked by one house and shop after another. On Street 294, he got lost. A man sitting in a chair outside a prosperous-looking house, evidently a security guard, looked up as Kamal walked by. Kamal asked directions. The man only belched and put his head back down.

The next road over, Kamal found Street 308, almost completely dark and deserted. The address written on the rumpled piece of paper was a fine two-story house, mostly hidden behind a wrought-iron gate, with marble columns on both sides of the gate and glass-enclosed lanterns atop the columns. An engraved brass plaque gave the address. Kamal peered inside the gate. In the light of the lanterns, he could see Sophea's white Land Rover. He could also see a tiled patio and a garden that wound around a little dark pond. Two windows on the ground floor glowed from the light within. Above them, a dim balcony and more windows. For a moment, Kamal tried to imagine how much money such a house must cost. He glanced back at the empty street. The incessant sounds of the city had faded to a soft murmur. In his pocket, he turned the piece of paper over and over. Then he heard Sophea's voice from one of the windows. It was a voice he knew, and at the same time a voice he didn't know. He remembered his last conversation with her, in the wedding tent, every word that she'd said. And he tried to match that voice to the one that he heard now.

His eyes found the window, and he wondered if she might come into view, but all he could see was a moving shadow. What was she doing? Was she waiting for him? Was she alone in the house? He looked again at the car, almost as if he didn't believe he was in the right place. Should he knock on the gate? Would she even hear his knocking? After all, he was hours late. Perhaps she had decided he wasn't coming at all.

Or perhaps she would look out and see him in the light of the lanterns, walk across the tiled patio, and greet him. Would she ask him into her house? Or perhaps the original invitation had been only an amusement to her, a tiny excursion from her life in this marbled house with the car and the rich men. Kamal stood in the dark and listened to her voice. He looked again at the marbled house and the Land Rover. And standing there, he realized how foolish he'd been. He turned and stared at the street and saw how it narrowed and dimmed in the distance, until it merged with the dark houses and disappeared.

THIDA

∾

(2008)

Neither Thida nor her mother had slept for two nights when they boarded the bus for Phnom Penh. Thida still held in her hand the small gifts her friends had given her at dawn before she left in the oxcart for Praek Khmau—a wire necklace, a scarf, and a tin can filled with dried fish. Exhausted, she leaned against her mother's shoulder and closed her eyes. The bus was packed. They sat behind a man who clutched a half dozen live chickens upside down, their legs tied together by twine. The chickens pecked at Thida's bare legs. Without opening her eyes, she kicked at the birds until they left her alone. Then she squeezed her mother's hand. At the age of sixteen, she was going off to live far from home for an indefinite period, possibly years, to work in the sweltering Glory Bless Garment Factory on the outskirts of Phnom Penh. Her mother would accompany her to the city, then return to their village. Ryna had pleaded with Pich not to let this thing happen. She had spent the last night pressed against Thida on her sleeping mat, her arms tightened around her daughter, both of them sleepless and without words.

As the bus started up, a cloud of red dust floated in and remained for the entire trip. The bus was hot and filthy. Food littered the floor. In front, the chicken man began coughing uncontrollably. Still squeezing her mother's hand, Thida looked out the window and watched the rice fields go by, copper-colored and parched in this season, cows wandering by the side of the road, clusters of wood shacks, occasional pagodas, naked children squatting on the ground. A moto carrying three monks passed by with their orange robes flapping in the wind.

Thida looked at her mother and said halfheartedly, "*Mae.* Nita can help you."

"No," Ryna shouted, startling them both with the tone of her voice. "Nita should stay in school." Ryna's eyes moistened. "*Mi-oun. Mi-oun.* My precious daughter."

Thida opened her purse and looked at the one photograph she was taking to Phnom Penh, a crumpled picture of her and her mother in the village pagoda last ancestors holiday. In the photograph, mother and daughter are holding hands. The mother possesses a stillness far beyond the moment frozen by the camera. The daughter appears supremely happy. Not quite as slender as her mother, she wears a knock-off blue jean jacket Pich bought in the market at Praek Khmau, with good luck beads wound around the buttons. She also wears a hat, unusual for the people of her village, soft and shapeless but angled stylishly and blue to match the color of her jacket.

Thida wanted to feel her mother beside her every time she looked at the photo, just as her mother sat near her now. Since she'd been a little girl, Thida had been the daughter who followed her mother everywhere, did errands for her, helped her with the cooking and cleaning, brushed her mother's hair at night. She slept with her mother on the nights her father didn't come home. When other girls asked Thida to play by the river, she refused, saying that she needed to stay home to help her mother. Her sister Nita was smarter. Srey-pov was prettier. Thida didn't care. She was the oldest daughter. She was the one the spirits had chosen to take care of their mother. Without being able to explain how, she'd understood that she'd been chosen. It was her honor. It was her blessing. Now she looked at the photograph and vowed that she would sleep through the next years as if in a dream, like walking through the dark fields at night, and never complain. And when the dream was over, she would return to Praek Banan and her mother forever.

As the bus neared Phnom Penh, Thida closed her eyes again and imagined brushing her mother's long silky hair, much longer than Thida's own shoulder-length hair. The brushing brought Thida quiet and calm. The long silky hair, the strokes downward and downward and soft like a breeze moving over the river, and all the night sounds of the world removed to a small patch of air and then silent. Silence.

It was three harvests ago that Pich first noticed the problem with his rice fields. A month after transplanting, half the young rice shoots turned brownish yellow. Kamal and Pich had just arrived at the farm, at dawn, and the fields were a soft sienna in the dim light. At first, Pich thought that he was not seeing clearly.

"What the fuck?" said Pich, and he threw his bucket to the ground.

"It looks like some kind of fungus," said Kamal.

"Do you know what a fungus looks like?" said Pich. Kamal didn't answer.

"Then don't tell me it's a fungus," said Pich. "What the fuck."

Pich walked a half mile to his neighbor Rama's

rice fields, with Kamal following ten steps behind. The rice shoots there were a velvety green. "Rama has poisoned our rice," said Pich. "I never trusted that idiot."

The next day, Pich rode his moto to Praek Khmau and bought some fungicide. He and Kamal spread it on their fields. Over the following week, more plants turned brownish yellow, with white spots.

At the end of the week, he told the family. They were sitting at the table in the one-room house, the six of them, discussing Mr. Em's new moto, when Pich suddenly changed the subject.

"Remember 1998," said Ryna. "We'll get through this again."

"That was then," said Pich. Almost as if to punish his family, he disconnected the radio from the wires that ran around the perimeter of the room to the car battery in the corner. "That was then," he repeated, and lay down on his sleeping mat. "If Rama was behind this, he'll be sorry." Pich rolled over and talked to the floor. "I'll borrow some money from Rith."

"I'm going out," Kamal said quietly. He put on a shirt and climbed down the rickety wooden ladder that led to the ground, where his friends were waiting for him on the dirt road. Thida could see their dim forms in the twilight. Across the way, kerosene lamps flickered in some of the houses, perched on their wooden stilts.

Thida kissed her mother. For a moment, she looked into Ryna's eyes, trying to discern if the family was in real danger. Then she went behind the hanging sheet that separated the daughters' sleeping area from the rest of the house. Nita and Sreypov followed.

Pich hated borrowing money. He hated being in anyone's debt. So he sold one of their three oxen instead. It was the lame one, the one they called Old Bean, injured in an accident several years earlier. Old Bean brought in enough money to last half a year. Still, the family had to tighten their belts. Ryna stopped buying fish at the market. Once a week, her dear friend Makara brought them a chicken. Ryna rationed out bits of the meat to add to their rice and boiled the chicken bones to make broth. Then they began rationing their supply of stored rice. On Saturdays, the children picked up damaged and rotting tomatoes and fruits off the ground in the back of the market. But they were still hungry. They didn't complain.

The following season, the same thing happened to the rice plants. They turned yellow and died. Pich took six dollars out of the emergency money tin in Ryna's trunk, put the bills in his pocket, and disappeared for three days. When he came back, stinking and drunk, he lay on the ground under the house for another two days. While he lay there groaning, Ryna went to talk to Rith and borrowed money. She hid the money under a wood plank of the toolshed and took it out little by little.

The following year, as if by a miracle, the rice plants were healthy again. But the family was in great debt. They owed twelve hundred dollars, more than a year of their annual income. Rith, a scrawny man, but muscular, began showing up at the house asking for his money.

"You should never have borrowed money from Rith," Pich shouted at Ryna.

"Then how do we buy our food?" said Ryna. "And where were you for three days?"

Pich looked around the room, his eyes red and wild. "We'll have to sell some of our land. What else can we do? Do you see what stupid *Mae Wea* has made us do?" he said, pointing his finger at Ryna.

Ryna sat down on the bamboo floor with her hands covering her face. Thida knelt beside her mother and put her arm around her. "I'll get a job," whispered Thida. "I'll get a job in the garment factories."

"I won't let you," Ryna said gently. She held Thida's hand.

"Pisey did it," said Thida.

"No," Ryna said firmly. But Thida could see confusion and fear in her mother's eyes.

Pich was sitting on the floor next to an almost empty bag of rice. "Let her go," he said.

"We can't do this thing," Ryna said to her husband.

"If stupid *Mae Wae* hadn't put us in debt . . . Daughter can send us forty dollars a month."

"Please," said Ryna, all of her defiance now gone. "I'll go to the garment factory myself."

"We need you here," said Pich. "And you're too old."

Thida stood up. "I'm going," she said. She hugged her mother. Then she turned to her father. "I want to go."

The bus dropped Thida off in the Meanchey district of Phnom Penh, half a kilometer from Glory Bless. Immediately, she was bombarded by noise—the honking of cars, the shouting of street sellers, the roaring of motos gunning their engines. And the crush of people, far more people than she'd seen at Praek Khmau.

"My precious daughter," said Ryna. "I have no more tears." Standing in the crowded aisle of the bus, she held her daughter tightly as she'd done the night before. "You are my heart. Come back to me."

"I will come back," said Thida. "I will come back. I love you, *Mae*."

She hugged her mother and got off the bus. She mustn't cry. She must be strong. She was the chosen one. As the bus drove away, she watched her mother's face in the window grow smaller and smaller. Her two bags, tossed out of the bus by the driver, had landed in a pile of broken glass and discarded food wrappers.

"Thida? Are you Thida?" Several factory girls were standing at the bus stop. They wore orange bandanas covering their hair. "You look scared to death, sister," said the tallest one. She picked up Thida's bags and smiled. The factory girls were all pale, Thida thought to herself. But pretty. "Your skin is so white," said the tall girl, whose name was Sivlong. "Do you use cream?"

"No," said Thida. "I'm just lucky. My mother's father was Chinese."

"I wish I had skin like yours."

"Don't ever let Mr. Liu take you alone into his office," said another girl, whose face was splotched with acne. "He likes girls with light skin."

"He's a pig," said Sivlong.

"If he tries anything, tell him you're having your period," said the girl with the acne.

They began walking, but to Thida it seemed as if they were running.

The street smelled of urine and beer. After a few minutes, they entered a building as tall as five houses stacked on top of one another and began walking up the stairs, stepping over empty bottles and wrappers and food. Up and up. On the third floor, they went down a hallway and opened a door. "This is ours," said one of the girls. "Three of us sleep here. You'll make four." It was a small room, empty of furniture. Damp clothes hung from strings crisscrossing the room. In the corners were more piles of clothes, a rice cooker, sleeping mats, and a television. The walls were covered with pictures of movie stars. Immediately, the girls flopped on the floor and turned on the television.

Thida called her mother once a week. She said she was happy and safe. She told her mother about her roommates, Sivlong and Sreypich and Chandy, the huge buildings and shops, the assortment of foods and items for sale, the cars that occasionally went by with rich people inside. She did not tell her mother that she had to work eleven hours a day, six days a week. Or that the factory was crammed with hundreds of girls sitting elbow to elbow, so that there was no room to walk when she stood up, or that the air was stuffy and laden with fumes so that she got headaches and red welts on her face and sometimes fainted. She did not tell her mother what Mr. Liu called her whenever she didn't produce her day's quota.

Thida had entered her dream. She worked at her small sewing table in the dream, trying to let her mind remain vacant. Her hands were not her hands anymore, but little pink stones darting about. Under her table, her legs went numb. In the tiny room on the third floor of the apartment building, she watched television with her roommates without seeing. On Sundays, her day off, she washed clothes in her dream. It was almost pleasant, the dream. She drifted and drifted and didn't feel her body or her mind. Wakefulness came for a few minutes at the end of each month, when she carefully wrapped forty-five dollars in a piece of cloth and gave it to Davuth, a family acquaintance, to deliver to her parents in the village. Davuth, whose own daughters were married, always patted her on the head and said *"kon srey laor."* Good daughter. As soon as he left for the bus, the landscape lost color again, and Thida floated back to her dream. Sometimes, she saw her mother in her dream and herself brushing her mother's hair, and it was silent and calm. Let it stay, she said to herself. I am nowhere. At the edge of the dream was a small light that was home. It, too, would stay. Days and weeks went by. Then months.

When Pchum Ben came, the ancestor holiday, the factory closed for a week, and Thida took the bus back to Praek Banan for a short visit. But nothing seemed real. She didn't feel at home. Her house felt like someone else's house, her sleeping mat that of a stranger. As she recited the ancestor prayers with her family, it seemed like someone else was reciting the prayers. Even her dear mother did not seem like her mother. Her mother's words and her touch seemed automatic, as if repeating a memory. Thida had muddied her dream. She had jumbled the past with the future. Somewhere ahead was the future, when she could quit the factory and reunite with her family. In between was the dream. Better to stay in the dream. She should never have gone home. After the holiday, the weekly calls with her mother grew shorter. After a year, Thida could not remember a life other than the walls of the factory and the tiny room on the third floor.

Sometime in Thida's second year at Glory Bless, Cousin Boran met her as she was walking out of the factory. Thida didn't recognize him at first. It had been a long time since his last visit to her village. For a few moments, she stood back. Was it Boran?

"Thida. Little mango. You're all grown up." His eyes wandered from her head to her feet. He walked closer and smiled. Cousin Boran was as old as Thida's father, but he had a much younger face, with perfect, straight teeth. None of the men in Praek Banan had teeth like that.

Thida was trying to remember where Cousin Boran lived. Was it Siem Reap? Prey Veng? "Cousin," she said. "How did you know I was here?"

"Your father told me. I'm visiting Phnom Penh just

for a few days and thought I'd say hello." He picked up his leather travel bag. "Let's get something to eat, little mango. I'm hungry. It's been a long time. We can talk. You're a good daughter, working here to help Pich and Ryna."

Thida was remembering more. She recalled some of Boran's visits. He told jokes in the evening and once helped her father repair his oxcart. Memories far away. They walked to Sovanna's Café across the street. It was dusk, and a string of lights dangled from the awning over the white plastic chairs.

After they'd finished a big meal of fried fish and bok choy, more food than Thida ate in a day, Cousin Boran took a piece of paper out of his pocket and put it on the table. Thida was fully awake now. Cousin Boran was telling her something. "Little mango, your father owes me money," he said. "A lot of money." Thida studied the piece of paper. She couldn't read everything, but she did recognize her father's thumbprint and mark. "To pay back this debt," said Boran, "you'll start working for Madam Chheng. She'll give you a place to live and plenty of food."

"Is it a garment factory?" said Thida.

"No." Boran paused. He moved aside one of the plates. "You'll be with men. But Madam Chheng will take care of you. She won't let anyone hurt you."

Thida began crying. But she wasn't inside her

body. She saw herself from outside of her self. She saw herself crying. She stared at Cousin Boran, and then she stared at the other people in the café, strangers, and at the dangling lights overhead. She stared at her hands.

"You have to do this, little mango." Boran reached out and touched Thida's shoulder. "Madam Chheng will pay a lot for you, enough to settle your father's entire debt to me. And you can still send a little money home every month. It won't be forever, your job there." Boran lowered his voice. "It's a gambling debt. Your father gambles. He shouldn't do it. It causes him trouble." Boran carefully wiped his mouth with a napkin. "I wouldn't be bothering him, but I need that money. This has been arranged with him."

He paused and looked at Thida. "Don't you want to help your family?"

In her mind, Thida saw her father slumped over the ladder in the middle of the night, drunk, missing his shirt, calling up to her mother for help. So many times. She knew that he gambled, like Soma's father. He did crazy things when he was drunk. He yelled and said bad words. But this? How could he agree to this thing with Cousin Boran? Didn't he love her? He used to go walking with her by the river when she was a child. He held her hand. She remembered. She was his daughter. He was her father. He had brought her into the world, made a home for her. There must be some mistake, something she wasn't understanding. She took out her phone.

"I wouldn't call," said Boran. "Your mother doesn't know. Do you want her to know?"

Thida kept her eyes closed while Madam Chheng stuck her fingers inside her to verify her virginity. Two other girls sat beside Thida on the bench, naked like her from the waist down. One clutched a teddy bear. "You aren't pretty," Madam Chheng said as she wiped her fingers on her scarf. "But you're fresh. And you have nice light skin. What a sweet thing you are, Thida. Our Thida. Our *kon srey*." Madam Chheng began laughing. Her teeth were stained red from chewing betel nuts. When she was finished with her examinations, one of the older girls brought in a plate of mango and sticky rice and put it on the bench.

Thida was thinking that her life was over. Over for her, but not for her parents. They would live on, perhaps another twenty years or more. Dear Mother. Sweet Mother. And Father. She knew that their debts caused them suffering. Now their sufferings would end. Nita would continue with school, perhaps even go to high school. Sreypov, little Sreypov would grow up. Kamal would get married and have children. They would all eat good food. What did her life matter? She was nothing. In the next life, things would be better. But in this life, she was already a ghost, who had to play her part. She was the one the spirits had chosen. Now she understood more than ever. This was the way she must help her dear mother. Still half naked, she swallowed a piece of mango without tasting it.

How long had it been? Three months? Four months? Thida and two other girls squeezed around a table with a man who gave his name as Arun. His face was swollen and red from three rounds of beer. Beer for everyone at the table. Thida mixed hers with ice and drank slowly. Bits of noodle and tamarind fruit littered the floor beneath them. Another man, a Westerner wearing a hoodie, sat in the corner with a girl on his lap facing him. At Thida's table, one of the ladies had drunk too much and put her head down. What was his name? Arun? You had to remember their names. His nose curved like a rice sickle. Curved into the curve of his face, which was a dim red moon in the dark night. Thida stared at the moon. He put his arm around one of the girls, who moved closer and slid her hand between his legs. A red sash hung on the wall and dipped down to the bar. Across the room, several girls perched on the bar stools wearing high boots and blouses bulging weirdly from cheap padded bras. A voice in the night fields: "Are you ladies feeling good?" Thida's eyes went to the mouth. The teeth gleamed with gold. What was it he said? One of the girls: "Doesn't she have nice boobs," and she pulled up Thida's blouse. Thida looked down. A hand fondled her nipples. "Who wants it? Or maybe I'll have all of you." The shape in front of her swung on the swinging steel chair and called to the woman tending bar. "How much for all three? I don't have much money." Thida looked at the man in the way that Madam Chheng had taught her. She smiled, but just a very slight smile with the corners of her mouth, and she looked directly into his eyes. Hold that for four, five seconds. Then look down at the table. Madam Chheng had taught her in the first week. Yesterday, Madam had come into her room and brought her perfume in a rose-colored bottle and some movie star magazines. "You keep your room nice," Madam had said. The black centers of her eyes were huge. "Honey, you have a bruise." She touched Thida's arm. "You're a brave girl. I got some ointment for your bruise." "Please," said Thida. "I'm OK." She was brushing her mother's hair and wanted to be alone. She liked being alone. She didn't smoke *shabu* with the other girls in the late afternoons. *Shabu* made them skinny and loud and the blacks of their eyes huge. Madam Chheng returned with the ointment and put it on Thida's arm, rubbing it back and forth. Madam began softly singing an old Khmer lullaby. "You have such pretty light skin," she said. "We have nice girls here." She began singing again. Deep from the cave of her dream, Thida's voice: "When can I go home?" "Go home?" said Madam. She kept rubbing. "You've been here only a few months. I paid a lot for you." Someone spoke. Was it the man at the table? The red sash dipped down to the bar. Thida smiled, as Madam Chheng had taught her to do, and she gave the man the look. Another round of beer. He'd already spent thirty dollars on beer. Madam Chheng sat at the bar in her tight "New York" T-shirt and signaled that the man could last one more round and then they should take him upstairs for boom-boom before he was too drunk to take off his pants. He would have to pay twenty dollars apiece.

Thida couldn't remember when she first started calling Madam Chheng by the name Auntie. A few of the girls, the ones allowed into Madam Chheng's room, called her that. The light from the declining sun struck the draperies in Auntie's room, streamed from one end to the other, and lit up the porcelain vase on the table. It was a large room, several times the size of Thida's room. It had a standing closet with beautiful clothes.

Thida sat on the sofa brushing Auntie's hair.

Below the draped windows, two young girls not older than eleven or twelve sprawled on the floor putting nail polish on each other, giggling, taking turns with the dozen or so tiny glass bottles on Auntie's bureau, the purples and oranges and reds. The bottles tinkled when they touched, making a musical sound. Another girl, wearing only her underwear, fluttered about the room dancing to the radio. Satya. She was the prettiest of all of them, and she let everyone know it. Even so, she was constantly putting her arm next to Thida's, comparing color and complaining about Thida's good luck. Satya came from a family of nine siblings in Mondolkiri. Auntie saved Satya for the wealthiest clients. They took her to the Intercontinental, and sometimes to the Raffles, where she ate fancy food in a room with chandeliers and swam in a pool. Or so she said.

These special girls, the ones allowed into Auntie's room, were now Thida's new sisters. Kimhuoy, Soren, Satya, Chanra, Sreyrath. They sometimes ate together in Auntie's room. They watched television in Auntie's room. Thida thought that she loved her new sisters, but she didn't love them completely. They made her think of her real sisters at home, in Praek Banan. When she talked to her mother, she didn't ask about her real sisters. That was the life of the past. She didn't tell her mother about Madam Chheng's. "Mr. Liu has gotten us new sewing tables," she said, lying. After each call, she couldn't remember anything that had been said.

"Look what I found at the riverside," said Soren, the oldest of Auntie's pets. She held up her arm to show off a bracelet.

"Found? Or slipped from some dumb cow?"

"Did you get my cigarettes?" murmured Madam Chheng from her place sprawled on the couch. One of the girls opened her purse and handed Auntie a package of cigarettes and a thousand-riel note.

Thida had twice been to the riverside herself, sent to lure rich clients, the ones with Apple phones and real leather sandals who paid fifty or even one hundred dollars for sex. Sometimes, the men came back to the brothel; more often they went with the girls to the Niron Hotel on Sisowath. Auntie let some of the girls out from time to time, the ones she trusted, the ones in great debt. They knew that if they tried to escape, Auntie would find them and have them beaten.

"You're pulling my hair," Auntie barked. Thida stopped brushing. She felt bitten. Auntie loved her special girls, but she still bit them.

"I want a cigarette," said Soren. She puckered her lips.

"No smoking in my room, honey," said Auntie.

"Mr. Hang comes here, and Mr. Hang doesn't like the smell." Auntie's special girls, her pets, knew about Mr. Hang. He'd been Auntie's boyfriend for the last year. Thida once saw Mr. Hang late at night. She saw them together, Auntie and Mr. Hang in the hallway walking toward Auntie's room. Mr. Hang had looked at Thida in the male way and touched her breasts as he passed. Auntie whirled around and slapped Thida hard. "Don't you fool with Mr. Hang," she shouted. "Do you hear me?"

Before Hang, Auntie had been married for a while to Mr. Mok. He had once owned a moto dealership on Russian Boulevard and could recite most of the *Reamker,* Auntie said. One day, Mr. Mok disappeared into thin air. "I think he had another family in Kratie the whole time he was fooling with me," said Auntie. "Men are cow shit. Even Mr. Hang. He slobbers all over me." These stories and more Auntie freely told as she lay drunk or drugged on her couch, the red betel juice dribbling from her mouth and her pets gathered about her. According to Auntie, her father had been a tour guide in Siem Reap and could speak English and French. In the late 1960s, before the war, he moved the family to Phnom Penh. How he earned money there, nobody knew. During the Pol Pot time, when everybody was forced out of the city, the family was split. Auntie was just a little girl then, but she still had sores on her legs from standing in water for hours. In one of the camps, Auntie's mother and two brothers died of starvation. Her father was last seen at the Thai border. All that remained of the family were her older sister and her. After the war, they came back to Phnom Penh and lived on the top floor of Lovely Molina's Bar on Street 172. Then her sister took ill with malaria and died. Every time Auntie told the story of her life, it was a bit different. In one version, her father was killed in the camps and it was her mother who fled to Thailand. In another, one of her sisters survived and was now living in Long Beach, in the United States. "Don't feel sorry for me," Auntie would say at the end of each rendition, and raise her head to see who was listening. "We have a family here. This is my family."

The girls constantly gossiped about who would be allowed into Auntie's room, who would become her next pet. The pets got better food and sometimes their choice of the customers. When Thida first arrived at the brothel, the girls began whispering about her light skin. Everyone was saying that Thida would become one of Auntie's pets. But Thida kept her distance. Auntie had a rough laugh, and she slapped. In those first months, Thida was completely silent, living in the land of the dead. The other girls, Auntie, the cook, Auntie's business partner Samphors, who carried a gun in her purse, the fat men and the skinny men—all were nearly invisible to her, pieces of flesh that made noise.

One night in September, when the rain was coming down hard and business was slow and the girls sat in the bar reading magazines, Auntie asked for a Coca-Cola from her table in the corner. Thida brought it to her. Just that small thing. Auntie reached up and gently touched Thida's cheek. Thida's breathing stopped. The music stopped. The laughing at the bar. The air. Thida had never felt a touch like that. This wasn't the hand that slapped. She floated. She covered Auntie's hand with her own. Her body dissolved into that loving hand on her cheek. "Honey, you're crying," said Auntie.

After that night, Thida began doing small errands for Auntie, bringing her drinks, following her around in the lounge and in the cooking area behind the brothel and in the cleaning room where they washed sheets. One night, she gave Auntie a bath in the kitchen, something she'd never done with her own mother, sponging Auntie's back with hot water while Auntie moaned with pleasure. Auntie's flesh turned pink and softened to Thida's touch. It softened and spread and warmed until Thida felt that she was part of Auntie's body. "My father sold me," Thida said quietly. "Men are shit," said Auntie. "I treat you nice, don't I? I treat you nice."

A week later, Thida waited in the hallway at night

in the dark until Auntie came out of the bathroom in her robe. There was a chance Auntie might talk to her there in the hallway, say something sweet, just the two of them. That was the first night Thida slept in Auntie's room. When she entered, two other girls were asleep on the floor. She lay down in Auntie's bed. But on the side nearest the door, in case Auntie turned mean.

Ryna was on the phone, crying and talking crazy. "*Mi-oun*, you have to leave that bad place. Come home right away." After a year of getting Thida's cloth packages of money from a third party, Davuth had grown suspicious and discovered where she was actually working.

"Are you getting the money?" said Thida.

"You have to come home."

"I can't. Madam Chheng paid seventeen hundred dollars for me."

"What! Who did she pay?"

"Cousin Boran."

"Boran!"

"Father owed him money."

Thida heard screaming and her mother and father shouting at each other. Then her mother got back on the phone. "I'll come get you," she said. "I'll be there tomorrow."

"No," said Thida. "Don't. Don't. If I try to leave, they'll hurt me. They might hurt you, too." She ended the call.

Thida felt herself shaking and couldn't stop shaking. Sister Sreyrath wrapped her arm around her. "What was that?" said Sreyrath, who had just put on her lipstick for the night.

"Nobody," said Thida. She took a long draw on the pipe.

"Was it your mother?" said Sreyrath.

"I didn't want her to know," said Thida, rocking back and forth. "I didn't want her to know. I didn't want her to know."

"The world is full of shit," said Sreyrath. "But we're beautiful, aren't we." She held a mirror to her face, and then to Thida's face. Thida looked in the mirror. The skin was thin and stretched tight, the eyes sunk in their sockets, the pupils huge.

"My mother won't love me now," said Thida. She put the pipe aside and lay down on the sofa.

"I don't have a mother," said Sreyrath. She kissed Thida on the lips. "We're all right here. We're beautiful."

"We're nothing," said Thida.

The third time that Thida's hymen was resewn to make her like a virgin again, she came down with a fever. It was her second year at Madam Chheng's. For three days, she lay burning on her bed, unable to get up. Several of the girls brought her cold soft drinks and noodles. Thida half opened her eyes and stared at the red fabric draped across the ceiling. Someone was holding her hand. "Sister." "Sister." In the distance, the sound of karaoke. Was it daytime or night? The room had no windows. It smelled of perfume, but underneath was the stink of the men. Someone grasped her hand. She was on fire. "Water." She opened her eyes. Auntie, on the edge of her bed, held ice to her cheek and stroked her forehead. Thida closed her eyes again. She was standing beside the river in Praek Banan with her little sister Sreypov and the river was orange, and then they were slowly paddling a fishing boat through the tall grasses. It started to rain. The rain soaked their clothes and felt cool and wet. Thida opened her eyes. Auntie was still there on the edge of her bed, holding ice to her cheek and softly singing:

> Sleep, my darling, sleep.
> Don't cry, my baby.
> Your rice with honey
> Is now prepared.

It must have been very early in the morning, because Thida couldn't hear any sounds except the call of the dawn noodle seller out on the street. Thida held Auntie's hand.

The girls brought her pills. When she got over the fever, she kept taking the pills. They helped her sleep. She would drift off, then wake up dreaming that a man was on top of her, even feel the weight and the sticky slime of him. In that twilight of sleeplessness and exhaustion, the room dimly lit by the bulb down the hall, she began to fully fathom what had happened to her. She'd been sold by her father. She'd been turned into filth. She'd look at the bottle of pills by her bed and think that maybe she should just swallow them all and be finished, like Soren had done. What did it matter? Wasn't she already dead? Worse than dead. In the dim light, she lay sleepless and stared at the pills.

The next night as she lay in her bed unable to sleep, the ghost of her grandfather softly entered her room. Ryna's father. Thida had seen the one photo of *Ta* that her mother kept in the small metal box. Grandfather appeared much older than in the photo, with little hair on his head and a limp, but he was easily recognizable from the missing front tooth and the narrow nose like her mother's. He carefully closed the door, so as not to make the slightest sound, and sat on the edge of the bed. Like all ghosts, he was translucent, so that Thida could partly see through him to the other side of the room.

"Granddaughter," he said. "You look like your mother." He patted her on the shoulder, and his eyes moved around the room. "Granddaughter, dear Granddaughter. I hate to see you in this bad place. Also, I hate to see you thinking bad thoughts. I've walked a thousand kilometers ten times to see this bad thing." "I'm sorry, *Ta*," said Thida. She thought to herself that she would tell her mother about this visit with *Ta*. But then she remembered that she would never see her mother again. "Don't do it," said *Ta*. "You'll get out of this bad place." "No," said Thida. *Ta* lived in the world of the spirits. He didn't know about brothels, the buying and selling of people, the debts, the filth. She looked at him again—an old man who didn't know much. "Listen to my words, *chao srey*," he said. "You'll get out of this place for sure." "I won't in this life," said Thida. "Just be ready to run," said *Ta*.

She put her head down and dreamed that she sat in the lounge with the girls, and it was so smoky from cigarettes that she couldn't see across the room. Everyone was coughing. When she opened her eyes in the dark, she too was coughing. And she smelled burning. For a while, she lay in her bed wondering if she was still dreaming. The house was silent. She must still be asleep. Then she heard a scream. "Fire." Suddenly, people were running down the hall. Someone flung open the door to her room. Smoke poured in. Thida rushed into the hallway, coughing. All the doors were open and the floor was wet. Should she go right or go left? At the end of the hall on the right was a narrow stairway barely wide enough for one person. Through the smoke, she could see several girls standing there with bags and photos ripped off their walls. Why were they waiting? On the left was a metal door leading to steep metal stairs winding down to the street two floors below. Someone wailed. "Get out! Get out!" Two girls came down the wood stairs from a higher floor dragging a third girl. Now Thida could see flames in one of the rooms and flames leaping down from the hall ceiling. She could feel the heat on her face. It was so hot. It burned. "Go down," someone screamed.

Thida ran toward the stairway, tripped over some bedding in the hallway, got up, and started down the stairs. Several girls rushed ahead of her. Her lungs burned, burned. She could barely see through the smoke. Auntie. "Where's Auntie?" she shouted. She saw Sreyrath at the end of the hallway. "Where's Auntie?"

"I think she's already out," said Sreyrath, running for the stairway. "Don't worry about her."

On the first floor, Thida ran down the hallway to Auntie's room. It was filled with smoke, and one of the walls was on fire. Auntie lay on her sofa coughing. When she saw Thida, she propped herself up on one arm and said, "Help me, honey."

In the next instant, Thida imagined that she was lifting Auntie off the sofa, pulling her out of the room and down the hallway, then out of the building to the street, out to the good air where the girls stood crying and safe under the blinking neon sign. "Help me," Auntie said again, pleading this time. For a moment, Thida stood there at the door, looking at Auntie coughing on the sofa. Then she turned and ran.

People in Praek Banan say that in the early mornings, you can see spirits floating in the mist over the river or hovering in the fields where the land meets the sky. Sometimes at dawn, the procession of monks going down to the river pauses for a few moments. "Listen," whisper the monks. "Can you hear them singing? We are blessed." Babies born during these spirit visitations are said to bring good luck from previous lives.

Every morning at dawn, just after the monks' procession, Pich and Kamal set out for their fields to tend to their rice and cucumbers and beans. They are still poor, but their debts have been paid, and Pich has begun speaking less roughly than in the past. But his daughter Thida will not look at him.

For anyone who asks, Pich and Ryna say that Thida spent three years working in the garment factories like a good daughter and now has come home. Over those three years, many of Thida's friends married. Soma But wedded Chanty Lov's son, and the couple built a house with a new tin roof near the monks' quarters in back of the pagoda. Kanha married a cousin in Takeo and moved to his family's sugarcane farm there. Kimsrung married a boy in the Phal family, who owns the spice shop next to the market. Already, Kimsrung has two children. A year ago, Thida's own sister Nita was married off to a rubber merchant and now lives in Battambang, far from home. Thida herself can never marry.

When Thida's friends invite her to come to their houses or to stroll with their babies, she declines. She is needed to help her mother, she says. When she sees friends at the market, she pauses to say a few words, but she never says much. Since coming home, she has been mostly silent.

At night, she sleeps with her mother. For some time now, Ryna has stopped lying next to Pich. Each evening before bed, Thida brushes her mother's long silky hair, the strokes downward and downward and soft like a breeze moving over the river. But some nights, she drops the brush and begins screaming. And even though she throws her arms around her mother's neck and locks their bodies tightly together, she sees Auntie staring at her from the sofa. The eyes slice through her like knives. And next to Auntie on the sofa is her father. He looks at her without expression, his hand cupping one of Auntie's bare breasts. At the same time, he is here, here, just on the other side of the hanging sheet. It is her terrible secret, the secret within the secret. It is the death without chance of re-birth. She sees the draperies on fire, the bureau on fire, the porcelain vase on the table.

PICH

⌒

(1973)

For a year, Pich had a job selling sugarcane after
school. It was a stupid job to pass the time and give
him a little cash to buy palm wine and occasionally
take a bus to Praek Khmau. One morning he woke
up and realized that it was mostly women and girls
who sold sugarcane. His mother sold sugarcane. His
cousin Riya sold sugarcane. Pich decided that his days
selling sugarcane were over. But he needed a little income. His half-blind brother Chann worked on the
family farm with their father, but that was hard la-
bor. Around that time, his one and only friend, Leap,
just before he left for Malaysia, told Pich that the easy
money was in stealing bicycles. So Pich began stealing
bikes and selling them in nearby towns.

At first, Pich was just another teenage boy who would sneak into some village in the middle of the night and try to wheel away somebody's bike from under their house—often stirring up the chickens and waking the family. But then he met a gang of young bicycle thieves. He didn't have any money, so he paid them two stolen chickens to let him join the group. Anybody can steal chickens, they said.

Pich needed practice if he was going to work with the gang. At night, he tried folding up the kickstand of his own bike a few dozen times, very quietly, then wheeling it out to the road. In the afternoons, he began studying old man Chea, who could walk around as silent as a light breeze.

After a month, Pich had some techniques figured out. The gang met every Tuesday evening next to the pagoda. They sat in rickety plastic chairs they took from Phirum's filthy restaurant. For an hour or two, they played cards and drank, and then they set out for the night's work.

It was a thrill, stealing bicycles in the moonlight. The boys dressed in dark clothes and signaled one another with their own invented sign language. They got to know all the sleeping villages along the Bassac. They'd ride past kilometers of dark rice fields, tangles of low scrub brush and palms, their bikes kicking up clouds of dust, and then they'd see a cow or two wandering on the dirt road, and the dim lights of a village ahead. If there weren't any soldiers on the road, the gang feared nobody. They could do anything they wanted. Sometimes, the boys snatched a sickle or a bag of rice just to show they could. But it was the bicycles they were after.

Occasionally, Pich would think about the victims sleeping up in the houses while the boys stole their bikes in the darkness below. If it looked to be an especially poor family, he'd pass that house and go to the next. After all, he told himself, he could steal only one bike on an outing. Most of the time, he didn't give a second thought to the owners of the bicycles. They had their business, and this was his business.

Pich didn't consider himself the brightest of the gang members, but he was good at pinching bikes. Some of the boys had a knack for theft, and some were skilled at sweet-talking dumb farmers into paying a thousand riels for a used bike. Pich was good at both. Within a couple of months, the other boys were following him around, studying his technique. Pich loved all of that. He was one of them now. For the first time in his life, he was a member of a group. He had friends.

A few of the boys had no talent at all. They couldn't keep from farting even right under somebody's house in the middle of the night. Or they would forget to bring along a tire pump. How could you steal a bike fifteen kilometers from home and not bring along a tire pump? Those boys were kicked out of the gang. They were endangering the operation. Go sell sugarcane, the gang's boss, Vann, told them. Yeah, go sell sugarcane, Pich repeated. The wannabe thieves threatened to tell their parents, and then Vann made his own threats. As far as Pich knew, nobody told their parents about the bike business. His own parents didn't care a cow's shit what he did. They never asked when he was coming home or where he'd been or where he'd gotten the money to buy a nice radio and a new bike. With Chann, they'd ask how many times he took a piss that day.

The most clever members of the gang were Vann and Dara. Vann didn't have a father. Eighteen years old, two years older than Pich, Vann was extremely handsome and always boasting that he had two girlfriends. He was planning to get rich and take the ladies to Phnom Penh and buy a big house for all three of them to live in like one happy family. Dara had a father, but his mother had died of tuberculosis, and he was passed around from aunt to aunt a few months at a time. One night, he told Pich that he'd never had a friend like him before. Me neither, said Pich. Leap was gone, but now he had Dara. They were lying on their backs under the tamarind tree near Pich's house, drinking palm wine and looking up at the stars. At that hour, most of the villagers had snuffed out their candles and lamps, and only one tiny light in the salt seller's house spoiled the perfect black of the sky. Somebody like you, said Dara, you must have lots of friends. Not really, said Pich. Then Dara said that he thought Pich was more than a friend, and he gently eased his hand onto Pich's thigh. Pich sat up and removed Dara's hand. Sorry, said Dara. I'm just drunk. Don't fucking do that again, said Pich, drunk or not.

With the bike business going well and no family duties except to pasture the family cow, Pich had time on his hands. He washed his new bike every afternoon, dirty or not. Sometimes, he met people to play cards. He usually lost at cards, but no matter. He had good money coming in. When he wasn't playing cards, he hung around the market. He would stroll past the bright red rambutans, the green morning glory, the squawking chickens with their feet tied together, and he'd steal a few items here and there, to keep in practice. He never stole anything from his cousin Bona's gasoline stall. One of the girls who worked in the fish stall started giving him the look and talking to him when he passed by. He liked her hair and her ass. On

Wednesday afternoons, he took her out to Khean's fields. She always wanted to talk, but he just wanted her to shut up while he got on top of her.

Pich was also thinking of dropping out of school. The school was a long yellow building with a red tiled roof and three classrooms made of concrete walls and concrete floors. No one had the money to maintain it, and the walls had holes as big as fists. Furthermore, all the shade trees had been cut down for firewood. Inside the school, it was unbearably hot. Pich would doze off, half listening to the teacher read from a French grammar, and wake up in a pool of sweat. School was a waste of time. School didn't help get a job. Nobody got a job, except for the farmers and sellers. And they were all poor. With the bike business, he had a good thing going.

He was thinking that finally his luck had changed. He deserved some good luck. So far, he'd had only bad. For one thing, he didn't look anything like his parents, and that was definitely bad luck, or maybe something worse. His brother, Chann, had the mouth of their mother and the chin of their father. Their sister, who died of malaria when she was three, looked exactly like their mother. But Pich didn't look like any of them. His parents used to joke that they didn't know where he came from. They would say it like maybe he was somebody else's child, or maybe not even Khmer. When his sister died, they made him stand inside a circle marked with chalked drawings of crosses and skulls. When he was thirteen, he ran away from home. But an uncle found him in Praek Khmau and slapped him so hard he fell to the ground, then brought him back to his family in Praek Banan.

Now he was showing them. Some mornings, he would leave a five-hundred-riel note lying on his sleeping mat just so his parents would see it. His father wouldn't say anything, but Pich knew that he noticed. Chann noticed too. Pich saw how his brother looked at his new bike. Chann's ten-year-old one-speed was always breaking down with a loose chain or a flat tire or something.

"What did you pay for it?" asked Chann.

"Enough," said Pich.

"You should have bought a Japanese."

"This one goes fifty on the national road."

"Really. You ever ride it that fast?"

"Yeah."

Chann nodded. "I like the color."

"The shop in Praek Khmau had them in gold and in red," said Pich.

"I like the red, the one you got," said Chann. "That's a lot of money you're riding. Stolen money."

"Money is money."

"I work for my money."

Pich was thinking to himself how much work could Chann do, blind in one eye, but he let it go.

After a year in the bike business, the boys were making as much money in a month as their parents made in half a year and were talking about extravagant plans for the future. Except that they had to hide in the shed in Khean's fields every few weeks, when Lon Nol's army came to the village in the middle of the night waving guns and looking for new recruits. Keep their heads down, Vann said, and they'd be all right and the war would be over and they'd all be rich.

With things going well, Vann decided to have a small celebration. He also decided that the celebration would be at Pich's house. Pich explained that his father was not a friendly man and definitely not enthusiastic about parties in his house. But Vann insisted. He said he would bring along enough palm wine to make everybody happy. A gift from him, he said. Vann had a way of talking so that you knew you should do what he said.

The party started around seven in the evening, when the fields were just turning purple and dissolving into the night. All along the main dirt road, you could hear the women and girls singing while they scrubbed dishes and tossed the dirty water out the windows. Some of the boys had already been drinking and could barely climb up the rickety ladder into Pich's house. It was a one-room house with two chairs and a table, illuminated by a kerosene lamp. In a corner sat a ten-kilo bag of rice and several sleeping mats.

Right away, Pich's mother, Layheng, drank two cups of palm wine, one after the other. Then she sat in one of the chairs, dazed. "I'll go with you to Naron's shop tomorrow," she said to Chann, trying to whisper.

"You don't need to, *Mae*," said Chann. "I'm just picking up hinges."

"I want to," said Layheng. "I'll keep you company." She patted Chann on his cheek.

"Tomorrow's wash day," said Pich's father.

"I know," said Layheng. "I can do the wash in the afternoon."

"I doubt that," said Pich's father. He winked at the boys. Then he turned to Chann. "You're right. You don't need your mother to go with you to Naron's shop tomorrow."

Layheng got up from her chair and went behind the hanging sheet that marked off the sleeping area.

After that, it was just the guys. The room was boiling hot, and everyone was sweating pretty heavily. Pich's father sprawled in one of the chairs without his shirt and poured himself a cup of palm wine. The boys were all sitting on the floor, passing around a bottle and listening to a song on the radio. Dara found a spot next to Pich, not too close but not too far away either.

"This music is crap," said Vann. "Let's play cards." He handed the deck of cards to Chann, on his blind side, and the cards fell on the floor. Chann started picking them up.

"You boys are going to get your butts caught," said Chann. He squinted at Pich with his good eye and took a large gulp of palm wine.

"We're professionals," said Vann.

"That's right," said Pich. "We're professionals. And you don't know shit about anything except shoveling shit." That brought a laugh from the gang.

"Chann's a good farmer," said Pich's father. "He'll take care of his family." In fact, Chann was engaged to marry Phalla, one of the most beautiful girls in the village, prized for her delicate features. Everything had been arranged. For some reason Pich couldn't fathom, girls were always falling in love with Chann. Some way he had of talking to girls.

Maybe they felt sorry for him. Pich looked over at his older brother. He felt like taking a couple thousand riel out of his pocket right then and laying it on the table. He fingered the bills.

The boys began talking about the war and when it would end. Some of their friends had been forced to join Lon Nol's troops and go north to fight the

Vietnamese. Last week, they'd seen a hundred troops on the national road. One of the boys heard on the radio that a bomb had fallen on Kol Phan and destroyed half the village. It was an army called the Khmer Rouge that launched the bomb, not the Vietnamese. Some monks were murdered after that.

Pich was half listening, mixing his palm wine with some beer he'd gotten from a bar in Praek Khmau. Although he was small and skinny, he could hold a lot of liquor. And he had experience. When he knew he was almost drunk, he ate some rice to dilute the alcohol in his body. He didn't want to puke in front of the group. Later, he was planning on showing them his pistol, which a cousin had taken from a dead soldier and given Pich for a present. He'd practiced shooting it at tin cans in the fields.

Pich's father went down the ladder to take a piss. He'd already helped himself to an entire bottle of palm wine. As soon as he was gone, Vann started in about his two girlfriends, Ratha and Maline. Maline's tits were so big, he said, that he thought they were fake, until he saw her naked. Even then, he had to put his hands all over her to make sure. She *asked* him to put his hands on her, he said. It was true love. Vann was leaning against the sack of rice, his face red from the alcohol. Ratha had small tits, he said, but her nipples were nice, like the buds of lychee flowers. Just last night, she'd given him a love bite on his shoulder. He took off his shirt to show everyone. They were in the middle of doing it, he said, and she just couldn't control herself. He lifted the kerosene lamp off the table and held it up to his shoulder, so the other boys could see the love bite. It was a red splotch, about the size of a small mango. It really hurt when she bit him, he said, but it was the kind of hurt that he liked. Vann bragged a lot. Pich suspected that sometimes he made things up. Vann took another long swig of the palm wine. Half the wine dribbled out of his mouth and trickled down his bare, skinny chest.

"Dara, what do you think of all that?" said Pich. "What Vann's talking about." Pich's head was beginning to hurt.

"I don't think anything about it," said Dara, slurring his words.

"You ever seen a girl's tits?" said Pich. Dara didn't say anything. He just took another drink of palm wine.

"I bet you've seen plenty of cocks," said Pich. That brought another round of laughter.

Dara crawled over to a corner of the room and began puking. His puke dripped between the bamboo strips of the floor and landed on the ox below.

Pich's father came back into the house. "It's time to go," he said. He looked over at Vann. "It's time for you gangsters to leave."

"They'll go," said Pich.

"What friends you've got," Pich's father said, slurring his words. "Fucking idiots."

"OK, OK," said Vann, "I'm gone." Vann made a monkey face to Pich and finished the wine in his cup. Then, without bothering to clean up the empty bottles and spilled palm wine and scattered mango pits, he stumbled down the ladder into the night. The other boys followed. Pich looked out the window and could see their dark silhouettes, pissing on the dirt road beside his house.

About a week after the party, the ghost of Pich's grandmother Pha appeared on the west hill. It was late afternoon, and Pich was bringing home the family cow when he met her. *Yeay* Pha looked exactly as she had in life, except now she didn't have any teeth, so that when she opened her mouth it appeared like a dark hole in her head. And she was much thinner. Slung around her neck was a ratty *krama*. Meeting ghosts at any time of the year other than Pchum Ben was usually bad luck.

"*Yeay?*" was all Pich could say. Grandmother? He came to a halt. His cow continued meandering down the hill.

"Yes, yes," Pha said, and coughed. "Grandson." She walked around him, eyeing him with concern, then sat on a flat rock. "You don't look good, Grandson. You're looking scrawny." Her voice sounded funny with the teeth gone.

Pich shrugged his shoulders. He was afraid to say much. Ghosts appeared for a reason. Had he insulted his *yeay*? He began thinking about the corner in their house where they kept photographs of her and Grandfather Sieng and the weekly ancestor prayers they hurried through before dinner.

Pha sat very still, as if she were meditating, except every now and then she swatted at a mosquito. She was planning on saying something to him, he could tell. Maybe she was waiting a while for dramatic effect. In his mind, Pich could see her sitting on the floor of the cooking area in their house, her usual spot, her bony legs crossed one over the other with the crusty white warts on both feet, mercilessly plucking the feathers off a chicken while complaining about how painful it was for her to walk nowadays, and how Pich's mother had never learned how to cook. Sometimes Pha would grumble about the sexy photo of Dy Saveth that Pich's father had tacked to the wall, until one day she snatched the poster down and threw it into the river. A man shouldn't be gawking at two females in the same house, she said. At night, after dinner, Pha would go behind the dangling sheet where she slept and have Pich's mother massage her back for a half hour with coconut oil. Everyone could hear her moaning with pleasure. Then she would tell a fairy tale to Pich and Chann and kiss them good night. Two years ago, she'd passed away in her sleep, with a grin on her face.

"How old are you now, Grandson?" said Pha.

"Seventeen."

"Time passes quickly for the dead. Bad days we're in now. Everybody killing everybody." She looked at him. "You should eat more." Pha stuck out her bare feet. The warts were still there. "But you're making money. Your father should have moved to Siem Reap a long time ago when I told him. Cousin Manith had a rich silk business there. Your father wouldn't listen. Farming is for the stupid people. Our family goes back to kings. Did you know that? We were royalty."

Pich had always gotten on with *Yeay* Pha. They used to sit together underneath a particular acacia tree behind the market while his mother was shopping. This was the first time he'd heard that his family came from royalty. Maybe his grandmother was just making that up. She did look a little crazy. For a moment, Pich's eyes wandered down the hill. The cow was long gone. His father and brother would yell at him for sure.

"I don't get enough to eat, Grandson. I'm hungry, very, very hungry."

"I'm sorry for you, *Yeay.*"

"Every day, I just walk around in circles. Ten

thousand laps a day. I walk every day in circles. And I get nothing to eat. You're the prosperous member of the family. I have a job for you. Yes." Then, in a tired voice, Pha recited a grocery list: Two bowls of rice. One rambutan. One bag of water spinach. Two mangoes. Half a boiled chicken. "Every Wednesday afternoon before sundown," she said. "Here. On this hill."

Pich repeated the items. The chicken might be hard to come by on a regular basis.

"Do you understand?" said the old woman. "Every Wednesday. Don't disappoint me. You're the one I trust." She swatted at a mosquito.

Pich felt honored that Pha trusted him. She could have come to his father or mother or Chann. But he was not happy with this assignment. Wednesday afternoons, he had other business. And he was afraid that he might bungle the job. Bad things happened to people who disappointed the dead.

That night, he told his parents about meeting Pha on the west hill. His father and Chann were packing up bags of rice seed. Planting season was only a few days away.

"I don't want that woman in this house again, dead or alive," said Pich's mother.

"You can demand anything," said Pich's father, "but ghosts go where they want."

"I heard a rustling last night," said Pich's mother.

"It was Pha. I'm sure of it. She was coming to steal my new sarong from Phnom Penh."

"Grandmother was missing some teeth," said Pich.

"You do exactly what *Yeay* Pha says," Pich's father said to him.

"Ghosts can get angry," said Chann, "and do evil things."

Sure enough, two weeks later, Pich forgot to include the rambutan in the groceries he left on the hill. That night, the ox below their house was mysteriously freed from its tether, and it took Pich and his father half a day to recover the animal. Another week, Pich provided only one mango in the week's delivery, and the next morning they found a crushed dog at the top of the ladder right in front of their door. He knew that his parents blamed him. Every Tuesday, he started to get anxious, thinking he would forget something again.

"This job shouldn't be left to you," Pich's father said to him. They were sitting at a table at Phirum's filthy restaurant, underneath a fading poster of the great temples of Angkor Wat.

"But *Yeay* Pha came to me," said Pich. "She chose *me.*"

"I'll go with him to make sure," said Chann with a smirk. Pich's father nodded.

"She chose me," said Pich again. He got up from the table, shoving Chann's chair as he did so.

•

"*Yeay* Pha must be getting fat," said Chann one afternoon after they'd left the groceries on the west hill.

"Probably fatter than when she was alive," said Pich. "She probably can't walk one step now." The boys laughed. "Are you and Phalla planning to live in our house?"

"*Mae* wants me to," said Chann. "Father does too."

"You should have your own house," said Pich.

Chann nodded. "Maybe you can pay for it."

Several months after the celebration at Pich's house, the bike business started to slack off. They had a good inventory of stolen bikes, but nobody was buying them. Vann and Pich discussed the situation one afternoon at a bar in Praek Khmau called the Banana Leaf. It was a place frequented mostly by middle-aged men who wanted to get drunk and spend a few hours with pretty females. There were always a few young girls at the counter, showing a lot of flesh and big smiles. One or two of them would sit next to each group of customers and drink and eat with them and pretend that they were about to walk out with them and screw all night. Sometimes they did.

It had started to rain. The drops pinged on the tin

roof. "Fuck it," said Vann, putting down his glass of rice wine. "I don't know what's happened. Everything was going nice. In another year, I could have set myself up in Phnom Penh."

"Maybe everybody's scared, with soldiers all over the place," said Pich. He took a long drink from his glass and fondled the girl sitting next to him. She put her hand on his thigh. Vann ordered another bottle of rice wine and some *prahok*. They'd already drank a half dozen glasses between them and eaten two plates of tamarind fruit.

Vann didn't say anything for a while. He was thinking. Or maybe he was just staring at the table. Long ago, Pich concluded that sometimes Vann was really thinking, and sometimes it just seemed as though he was thinking. He wasn't as smart as he looked. Pich had never liked Vann. In fact, he didn't really like any of the boys in the gang. They all acted as if they were more clever than they were.

"Our business is over," Vann finally said. "Now I'm going to have to get some other job. I might have to sell vegetables. Or work on a fucking farm. Have you ever done that? You ever worked on your father's farm?"

"No."

"Well, you might have to. I had a dream about working on a farm. I was squatting in the mud, picking snails out of the ditches. Can you believe that? Me picking snails."

"You shouldn't dream," said Pich. He drained his glass of rice wine and ate a piece of *prahok*.

"Everybody dreams. It's good for you."

"Anyway, you still have plenty of money," said Pich. "You got twice as much as the rest of us."

"I spent it."

"Really? Ratha and Maline?"

Vann poured himself another glass of rice wine from the bottle. "You might have to work on your father's farm," he said. "Maybe I'll be working there with you."

"Yeah," said Pich. He was thinking about what Grandmother Pha said. That they were royalty.

"Maybe we should go to Thailand," said Vann. "I don't like this war going on. I heard of a guy who went to Thailand and was getting paid twenty thousand riels a month. What do you think?" Their two girls got off their stools and disappeared behind a curtain without explanation. Another girl was trying to wake up a man who had passed out, his face flat on the bar counter.

"Thailand?" said Pich. "But what about Ratha and Maline?

"Bitches. They're not around anymore. Fuck Ratha and Maline. You and I should go to Thailand and make some money."

"I'm not going to Thailand," said Pich.

"Come on. Go to Thailand with me."

"What are we going to do in Thailand?" said Pich. "You don't know shit about Thailand. I'm not going to Thailand. Why don't you ask Dara to go to Thailand with you?"

"Dara's joining the army. He's going to fight the Vietnamese. Or the Khmer Rouge. Whoever."

Pich was thinking about the time he and Dara lay under the tamarind tree looking at the stars and that Dara probably wanted to get himself killed. "I'll talk him out of it."

"Do what you want," said Vann. "I think he's already gone."

Their two girls returned to the bar counter, barefoot, holding another bottle of rice wine. As Pich's girl leaned over to nuzzle him, the room started to spin around his head. He stood up and sat down again. He'd let himself get drunk. "Shit," he said to himself. He reached into his pocket. He had only thirty riels left.

On the trip back to Praek Banan, Pich got sick. Twice he had to lean out the window of the bus to puke. When he finally got home, he couldn't climb the ladder up to the door, so he lay down in the hammock under the house, next to the oxen. He didn't bother taking off his clothes. The world was still spinning.

Fitfully, he drifted into a drunken sleep. Once during the night, he woke up to the sound of his father pissing in the bushes. "Father," he whispered. His father glanced over at him and went back up the ladder.

The next morning, it was still raining hard. Pich lay in the hammock. His head pounded. He didn't want to do anything today. He just lay in the hammock and listened to the rain. Turning, he saw that the road in front of their house was all mud. An oxcart had gotten stuck, and a man was trying to wedge rocks under its wheels. On the other side of the road, the houses on their stilts had disappeared. All he could see was a gray curtain of rain. Pich's parents and brother were up in the house. He could hear them talking—something about the bad crop last year and how they'd better have a good one this year to pay debts. He was hungry, but he didn't want to get out of the hammock, not when the ground underneath had turned into mud. A small river of water flowed down from the road, went under the house and out the other side. Pich inhaled a deep breath of the damp, humid air and watched a particular raindrop as it slowly slid down one of the wooden stilts of the house to the ground.

Later, his mother came out to go to the market. As soon as she reached the ground, her feet sank in the mud and left gaping holes, which quickly filled up with water. Chann climbed down the ladder and sat on the bottom step and began stitching a torn burlap bag. They weren't going to the fields today, he said. Tomorrow, they'd begin harvesting the cucumbers.

"You ought to get up," said Chann. "Lazy shit." He picked up a stick and slapped Pich on the leg. That insult couldn't go without a response. Pich got out of the hammock and found a stick of his own. Soon the boys were out on the road, thrusting at each other with their sticks as they'd done when they were kids. The rain was coming down hard. Their clothes were sopping wet, their legs covered with mud halfway up to their knees. With each step, the mud gripped their feet like hands holding on. They took off their shirts. The rain against Pich's chest felt like little fingers jabbing his skin. Back and forth they swiped at each other. Chann lunged forward and poked Pich's chest with his stick. Then he retreated. Pich advanced and struck his brother's arm. He looked toward their house. It had vanished like the other houses, inside the cave of the rain. He could hear the man with the stuck oxcart shouting at his ox but couldn't see him. Now the rain felt good on Pich's body. He felt as if he were in a cool dream. A mansion of water enveloped him. He was walking through mansions of water. Then he was floating. He lunged again. Somewhere, he heard a scream. It was Chann's scream. Through the curtains of water, he saw Chann fling up his hand to his good eye. Blood streamed down his face and mixed with the rain.

Pich rode in the bus with his parents and brother to the hospital in Phnom Penh. Since the accident, no one had said a word to him. It was as if he had disappeared in the rain. How had it happened? He went over the moment again and again in his mind. He could see them there in the rain lunging at each other. He could feel the rain in his mind. On the bus, he sat in the seat behind Chann, his hand on his brother's shoulder the entire two-hour trip. His mother didn't stop sobbing. Once, she turned around and looked right through him.

The next day, Pich's father said to him, "The devil is in you. You were born with the devil. We always knew."

For the next several days, no one spoke to him. I didn't mean to, he said over and over. No one spoke to him.

His parents watched silently as he began packing his clothes. He wanted to say something to Chann. What could he say? He touched his brother's arm. Chann flinched. Then Pich left. He moved in with his cousin Bona on the other side of the village. I didn't mean to do it, he told Bona. Bona nodded.

In a week, Chann began coming out of the family house. He went down the ladder slowly and gingerly, on his rear end, one rung at a time. He wore a white bandana around his forehead, covering both eyes. On the ground, he took small steps and held on to his father's shoulder. Sometimes his mother led him through the village, holding his hand. Sometimes it was Sna, the fruit seller. Whenever Pich approached, Chann's helpers waved him away.

Chann could no longer work on the farm. He started helping Sna in his stall at the market. Pich saw him there, taking rambutans out of a burlap bag and arranging them for buyers, each a bright red ball with spiny threads. Chann sat on a stool. He would reach into the burlap bag and bring out a cluster of rambutans. Then he would break them off at the stem one by one, feel around for the table and the other rambutans, and place the new ones next to them. He did the same thing over and over again. Pich watched from the tire seller's stall. He was obsessed with witnessing the destruction he'd caused. He wanted to wallow in the destruction, feel it cut through his body.

He had nothing to do now. He had no job and no money. He was living off his cousin. Most mornings, he would just sit outside Phirum's restaurant or watch the sellers set up their stalls in the market, then walk along the muddy main road past the pagoda, past the salt seller's house, and end up near his family home. He'd stand across the way for a few minutes, not sure why he was there. Maybe he should join the army. He looked across at his house, waiting for someone to appear.

One night, Pich dreamed that he was in a field full of water buffalo. It was after sundown, but he could see everything clearly. The water buffalo stood in a line by a flooded rice field, hundreds of them. He walked down the line and one by one slit their throats with a kitchen knife. Black blood sprayed from the cuts. Each butchered animal fell sideways into the flooded field with a splash. When he woke from the dream, it was still night. He looked up from his sleeping mat and saw that the walls of Bona's house were moving toward each other, and the kerosene lamp was casting the shadow of the Buddha on the palm-leaf roof, and the shadow was twitching this way and that. The walls of the room were coming closer and closer until they were only two meters away on all sides of him and they were still coming at him, about to crush him, and he couldn't breathe. He was sucking in big heaves of air but he still couldn't breathe.

Another night, he dreamed that he was digging a wide and deep hole in the ground near the pagoda. Again, it was dark. His shovel hit something at the bottom of the hole. It was bone. It was a skull.

Somehow, the skull was familiar. At that moment, his grandmother Pha appeared. She'd definitely put on weight. But she wore the same ratty *krama* around her neck as when he saw her on the west hill. She looked at him standing in the hole. Her face glowed silver in the moonlight. My little Pich, she said. Did you mean to do it? I don't know, he answered. Everyone else knows, she said. Pha reached out and placed her hand lightly on his shoulder, and he began crying. Little Pich, she said. He couldn't stop crying.

He remembered the dream in the morning as he sat eating rice and egg with his cousin. "You look tired," said Bona. "I haven't been sleeping well," said Pich. "Mosquitoes," said his cousin. "I'll get a net for you." "I'm all right," said Pich. "You can't be all right," said Bona. His cousin began washing a bowl with a tin can of rainwater. The water ran into a bucket. "You can work with me selling rice," said his cousin. "Mr. Dinh comes once a week with his truck to buy rice. As long as the cadres don't attack him on the road from Praek Chrey. You can help me round up the rice from the farmers." Pich nodded. He looked out the window at a procession of monks passing by in their saffron robes and yellow umbrellas.

That night, Pich walked to his family house and climbed up the ladder. He stood in the doorway. He could see on the table little packages of mango and sticky rice. Damp clothes hung from a string stretching diagonally across the room. His mother and father and brother were eating rice and dried fish. When his parents saw him standing there, they stopped eating. "The devil is not coming to this house ever again," said Pich's father. Suddenly, Pich didn't know what to do with his hands. They didn't feel like his hands. He put them in his pockets, then let them drop by his side, then put them in his pockets again. He stood there a moment. Then he left.

He didn't return to his family home until years later, when his parents were dead.

SREYPOV

(2015)

I.

When rice shoots turn brown,
Our bellies are emptied—
The Buddha has frowned,
And he loves us no more.

Mekh. Sky. That was the name she gave to her journal, written in blue ink on the first page. And underneath, her name, Eng Sreypov. Youngest daughter of Eng Pich and Srun Ryna. Embossed on the journal's cover was a luminous image of a Western woman with flowing gold hair, aglow with bright petals of flowers, and a child's face nestled in that hair. The journal had been a gift from a city cousin of Sreypov's mother, Ryna, who then gave it to Sreypov a few months after she turned thirteen. She was the only one of her friends who kept a journal. Those pale blank pages, into which she wrote poems as well as private thoughts, she cherished like her breath. She had begun writing poetry after her ninth-grade teacher required the students to memorize parts of the *Reamker,* recited in the burning mornings before the young scholars went home for lunch. Titles of some of the poems: "Blood Monsoon," "Twilight," "Starvation," "A Visit to the End of the World," "Mother Sleep," "Walking Through Night Trees." A newspaper devoted to Cambodian youth, *Samleng Yuvachan,* ran a competition for rural students and published several of Sreypov's poems.

From the beginning, it was a journal of both sadness and joy. The first page, written by the light of a kerosene lamp in the females' area behind the hanging sheet: "10 March 2011. Sister Thida came back a week ago. *Mae* and I waited in Praek Khmau two hours for her bus. I'm so happy she's back. I can't even remember what she looked like when she left. She's so skinny now. When I hug her, I can feel her bones. *Mae* is giving her coconut milk every day and sleeps with her. She hardly says anything. Also, she's afraid to leave the house. I told her that when *Mae* dies, I will take care of her. When I said that, she started crying.

She doesn't even look at Father. I know that he did a terrible thing to her. It is a shame of the family."

On a later page of *Mekh*, shortly after her sixteenth birthday: "17 May 2014: Sometimes, I can see the insides of my body. There's a solar system in there, with a sun and a moon and planets whirling around. I think it must have come from a previous life. Possibly I was a star before I became a human. I know that I am different from other people. I can feel light. Definitely. It's a tingle on my skin. I can also feel dark. When I feel dark, I am kind of excited, but scared. My stomach gets heavy."

It was at the age of ten that Sreypov began going outside at night to lie on her back in the rice fields and look up at the stars. At the time, the family had just endured two straight seasons of diseased crops, with barely two or three eggs to eat per week, and Thida had gone off to Phnom Penh to work in a garment factory. She didn't come back for three years. In those bad times, Sreypov's parents were always arguing over money, so she began slipping out of the house after dinner and walking to the neighboring fields, where she could find peace. Even at age ten, Sreypov liked to be by herself. At first, Ryna worried about the child's safety and tried to stop the nocturnal excursions. "I'll be careful, *Mae*,"

Sreypov would reply without slowing, and she'd continue down the ladder to the dirt road. Outside, she'd pass Mr. Noeum's house, with the bushy weeds growing in front and the broken moto, then Mr. Em's ghost-inhabited house on the other side of the road, Mr. Ly's house, Mr. Sen's house with a clothesline strung across his front yard, Makara and Sayon's house with the wire chicken coop in the back—all the houses glowing with kerosene lamps and an occasional electric light.

The men were all farmers except for Mr. Ly, who bought cheap motos from Vietnam and sold them in Praek Banan and the surrounding villages. Mr. Ly was the most prosperous man in the village. Some people wondered why he didn't move to Phnom Penh. Others said that he liked being a big fish in a small pond. One year, Sreypov helped Mrs. Ly with her shopping when she was ill, and Sreypov still received little gifts of fruit from her at the Khmer New Year. Every night, Mr. and Mrs. Ly's house was brightly lit with a string of electric lights, run off a big gasoline generator. The machine sounded like three moto engines going at once. When Mr. Ly's generator was cranking, nobody in the village could sleep, and all the oxen under the houses shifted and snorted. On her way to the night fields, Sreypov would put her hands over her ears when she passed Mr. Ly's house. She'd wind around the moon shadows of pigs and cow poops in the dark road, then on to Mr. Bayon's dry goods store, where there were usually some teenaged boys sitting outside smoking and playing cards by the light of a kerosene lamp. That's where she left the main road and headed south toward Mr. Hang's fields. In another kilometer, she couldn't hear Mr. Ly's generator or any sounds from the village. It was pure quiet, and pure dark. For the first month, she just stood there for a half hour, happy in the silence. Then she began lying down in a dry spot and looking up.

It was another world up in the night sky. After a few minutes, Sreypov would feel herself falling into that world. How far did it go? she wondered.

Lying there, she lost track of the animal sounds in the fields, she lost track of her body, she lost track of time. She just was. She saw patterns in the stars, not the ones she'd learned in school, but other patterns: trees and ships and crowns that princesses wore. Did each star know that it was part of a pattern? It must. And yet each star was alone, like her, a single point in the world. The stars were bright little eyes looking at her, the tiny spokes of light coming down to exactly the spot where she lay in Mr. Hang's fields and tingling her skin. She felt comforted by them, so quiet and confident and still. Yes, it was a stillness. The night sky was the mind of the Buddha. And it seemed that the vast expanse of time, going back to before her parents were born and before her grandparents were born and back and back through the generations that she never would know, and then going forward in time to when her parents would be dead, and she would be dead, on and on into the future—all of that unending strand of time seemed compressed to a dot. That single dot contained everything that was and everything that would be. She was that dot.

When Sreypov came out of the trance, sounds would appear in her mind. Eventually, the sounds turned into words, which later turned into poems.

"Why do you go out there at night, *mi-oun?*" her mother asked. "Once upon a time I was a star," said Sreypov. Ryna nodded and gave her daughter a kiss. "You are beautiful like a star." Then Sreypov would read Ryna her latest poem while her mother listened with closed eyes. "I want to be a poet," said Sreypov. "Like Krom Ngoy." "You will be," said Ryna. "You are the fire in this family. You are the fire."

When people in the village looked out their windows at night and saw the dim form of Sreypov walking back from the fields, she could feel their disapproval. They thought she was haunted and bringing bad luck to the village. Some told their children to stay away from Pich and Ryna's "strange daughter." You are you and I am me, Sreypov thought to herself.

To be sure, there was plenty of bad luck in the village. But Mr. Noeum couldn't blame her for the tree that fell on his tin roof. That tree had been sitting in a dangerous position for years, the trunk halfway sawed through by Mr. Noeum's crazy son, and everyone had been telling him forever to take it down. Or Mrs. Nol's husband, who disappeared one day during the Khmer New Year festivities wearing his new silk jacket and sandals from Praek Khmau and smoking an expensive cigarette. For the next week, Mrs. Nol gave Sreypov the hard suspicious stare in the vegetable stall. "Don't come near me," said Mrs. Nol, who wore wool sweaters even when it was ninety degrees. "You little *srey arak*, you little devil girl." "You don't know anything about me," said Sreypov. Husbands were disappearing all the time for one reason or another, she wanted to say, but she held back. She didn't want to make Mrs. Nol even more angry and upset. And what about the drunk lady named Grandma Lo-la, who cast spells on all the houses as the boys rolled her down the road in a wheelbarrow. Why not blame *her* for bad luck?

And what about the bad luck of Sreypov's own family? By far the worst bad luck was what happened to her poor sister Nita. Dearest sweet Nita. On 15 September 2014, she skidded into a tree on her moto, broke her neck, and was killed instantly, leaving her one-year-old daughter, Theary, to be raised by the family. Some of the villagers blamed Sreypov and her nightly wanderings even for that.

Sreypov tried to ignore all the mumblings and just go about her day. In the early mornings, she played with her little niece, already beginning to look like Nita. When her mother and sister went off to the market, she met her friends at the pagoda and walked to class in the four-room schoolhouse with the crumbling walls. After school, in the warm afternoons, she studied her history and biology and Khmer lessons, helped prepare dinner for the family. In the evenings, she went out to the fields and wrote in her journal. Many of the villagers couldn't write at all. Most hadn't finished eighth grade. Most hadn't journeyed a hundred kilometers from Praek Banan, or even as far as Praek Khmau, where Sreypov sometimes went with Kamal to the Internet cafés. There, she'd read about Aung San Suu Kyi and Hillary Clinton and seen a video clip of a soccer game in Brazil. Praek Banan was just a speck in the world. A thousand villagers in all, counting men, women, and children. They formed their opinions listening to the radio at night. In the day, those opinions were stretched and spun sideways and refashioned by gossip, mostly by the women walking in pairs to the river to do a wash or sitting in the shade under their houses while their husbands were off in the fields. They talked about how they were managing their husbands ("my husband won't eat anything but meat," "my husband hates me to fall asleep before him"); marrying off their daughters ("tell your daughter to wear a red wristband on her wedding night, and she'll get pregnant right away"); shopping ("Chinese people are owning everything these days"). Sreypov heard all the talk, but she kept it to herself. Except in her journal, where she wrote everything down and formed her own ideas. You are you and I am me, she thought to herself. Gossip and do what you want. Believe what you want. I'm a poet. I'm going to university. And after that, who knows what.

II.

As day moves to night,
Light fades and dims,
Death one day nearer.
I reach out my limbs
To the undying stars.

When Sreypov turned seventeen, Pich began planning for her to wed Mr. Ly's son, Kosal. Pich didn't say anything to Sreypov, but she heard him whispering to Ryna. "Mr. Noth never coughed up anything for us,"

Pich said to his wife late one night as they lay side by side under their mosquito net. "All that money, and nothing for us." "Poor Nita," whispered Ryna. "It was a tragedy," said Pich. "She was a good daughter. But we wasted the chance. Battambang is too far away. We shouldn't have let Daughter Nita go to Battambang. We have to marry Sreypov to someone closer, so we can keep control." "Daughter Sreypov isn't ready to get married," whispered Ryna. "She has one year left of school, and that's what she's going to do." "Listen to me," Pich said. "Sreypov is already seventeen. Ly is rich. And he's right here under our noses. We can keep an eye on him and his son. Sreypov is friendly with his wife." "Sreypov will not agree to it," said Ryna. "She'll do what I tell her," said Pich. "If you think so," said Ryna, "then you don't know your daughter." From her sleeping mat behind the dangling sheet, Sreypov smiled.

There was a page in Sreypov's journal, dated 3 October 2015, with some words scratched through, written again below, scratched through a second time, then finally written again. The words were: "I hate Father."

When Sreypov wrote those words, lying under the stars one night, she felt as if one of the planets in her abdominal solar system had suddenly exploded, spewing dirt and rock into space. Surely, she had just cursed her karma for the rest of eternity for even thinking such a thing. In her next life she'd probably come back as a bug, or a snake. But she'd thought it, and she'd written it, and she couldn't bring herself to scratch it out again. A kind of freedom swept through her, mixed with a dread. And a power. She felt powerful in the sacrilege and the clarity of the statement.

In *Mekh*, time didn't flow uniformly. Whole months went unrecorded. By contrast, some hours were split into second-by-second observations: tiny brown insects moving from one blade of grass to the next. Some entries skipped ahead, sprinkled with poems. Present and past sometimes merged, sometimes crossed, sometimes dissolved into the future. That was the way of memories and premonitions. "I hate Father," she wrote on 3 October 2015, when she felt that she'd started some big thing in motion.

But the thing had already started the previous night. She'd been on her way back to her family house after lying in the fields when she spotted the silhouette of her father out on the road. Immediately, she felt the dark churn in her stomach. But she followed him. He was walking in the direction of Khean's fields, a vast expanse at the edge of the village once owned by old man Khean but never farmed. After the Pol Pot time, newcomers to the village had begun building their houses on Khean's fields without asking anyone for permission, but no one objected. Sreypov knew her father's gait well—when he was setting out for his farm at dawn, when he was coming home tired at the end of the day, when he was drunk. But this night his shadow, framed by the light of the moon, moved in a way that she'd never seen before. He walked briskly, and there was something else unfamiliar and strange in his gait. Sreypov kept a distance back as she followed. He walked past the Cheam house, the Soy house, the Kim house, and the Yarn house, a group of families who had moved together to Praek Banan from Takeo. Their houses glowed in the night. Even though it was well past the evening meal, the smells of garlic and ginger and lemongrass hovered in the warm air. Just beyond those houses, Sreypov passed a broken moto on the side of the road. In a dark stretch, Pich stopped suddenly. Sreypov ducked behind a tree. Then he veered off the main road and walked on a narrow dirt path past another cluster of houses, approaching an isolated house beneath some tamarind trees. He climbed the ladder of that house, removed his sandals, and went in.

Standing in the moon shadows, Sreypov could see her father through the window. There was a woman. They embraced and kissed. It was a long embrace, more tender than any she'd seen with her mother. When the couple separated, Sreypov recognized the woman. It was Lakhena, her father's girlfriend of several years. Lakhena was well known to the family. Ryna had occasionally pointed her out to the children, referring to her as a dirty woman, but Sreypov had never before seen Lakhena's house. Somehow, she'd always imagined that Lakhena was part of a story that may or may not be true, perhaps just an acquaintance of her father—in any case a situation well beyond her understanding. But that kiss now, she had seen. Why didn't her father kiss her mother like that? For a few minutes, Sreypov walked about in the shadows below the house, unsure what she should do. Then she climbed the ladder and stood in the open door frame.

The room was lit by two kerosene lamps. On a table near the door, a bottle of palm wine and two glasses. Several meters away stood Lakhena and her father. He looked thinner than usual. For a few moments, no one spoke. So this is the place, Sreypov thought to herself, the place where Father goes one night a week, coming back to their house at dawn, disheveled and moody. This was the place. The room had his smell. Was this like a second home to him? Did he feel at home here? This man was her father, and at the same time he wasn't her father.

"Would you like to come in?" said Lakhena. She seemed to know Sreypov. She'd seen Pich together with his children at various events.

Pich's body stiffened. He looked at his daughter as if she belonged to someone else. "This is none of your business," he said. "Go home. Go back to your mother."

"You're my father," said Sreypov.

"Let your daughter come in," said Lakhena, as if they were all part of one big family.

"I don't want her to come in," said Pich.

"I'd like her to come in," said Lakhena. "This is my house." She took a step toward Sreypov.

"You have no business being here, Daughter," said Pich. "Never follow me here again. Now go home."

Sreypov walked into Lakhena's house. It looked much like her own house, except everything was extremely neat and in place. Perhaps Lakhena had just straightened the house especially for her father's visit, or perhaps it was always orderly. She saw two bowls of rice and vegetables on the counter, some mangoes, a woman's dress neatly folded over a chair, a shirt she recognized as her father's, a belt. For the first time, she became aware of the music, coming from a radio. The music added to the injury. Nearby, she saw the sleeping mats. For a moment, she imagined her father and Lakhena lying there together. Now her father was holding Lakhena's hand. She'd never seen her father holding *any* woman's hand.

"Father," she screamed. She looked at him straight in his eyes and kept staring.

"Lakhena takes care of me," said Pich. "Better than your mother does."

"Your father and I are good together," said Lakhena.

"You act sweet," said Sreypov, "but you're a bad woman."

Pich slapped her. Then he poured himself a cup of palm wine. He sat down in a chair and crossed his legs in an easy manner. "I work hard," he said to his daughter. "I sweat. I put food on the table. I take care of my family. I can do what I want. You're a child. You don't understand anything. Go home."

Later that night, Sreypov couldn't remember anything that had been said. She was shocked—by the slap, of course, which still burned, but much more by the realization that her father was capable of sweetness and love. Was it ever there with her mother? She strained to remember. She began thinking of other husbands and wives that she knew in the village. Some showed mutual affection, many did not. Why did people get married at all? Sister Nita hadn't loved her husband, she knew that for sure. Makara's husband beat her. Maybe she herself would never get married. Marriage was a trick. It wasn't what people said. She could never tell her mother about what she had seen. Maybe her mother already knew all of it, the sweetness and the dirtiness of it. As Sreypov lay on her mat, unable to sleep, a sadness went through her, and a fear. The world had grown unsteady and mean under her feet. She felt adrift. For some years, she'd imagined a life beyond Praek Banan, but she wasn't sure such a life really existed, or whether she deserved it even if it did. She was the blood of her parents, no changing that. She was a part of the lie. And she felt more suffering and darkness to come. Something.

III.

Sister flying through the night,
Her lovely life a thread so slight,
While blacker night stands still and waits
To crush a thousand lovely fates.

"I'm not going to marry Kosal," Sreypov said a few nights later. She didn't say it to her father. She didn't want to talk to him anymore. She just said it.

"Kosal!" said Thida. She stopped brushing her mother's hair. "He does nothing except play cards." Thida covered her mouth as soon as she realized she had stumbled into a family dispute she knew nothing about.

"How do you know about this?" said Pich. "Never mind. It will be a good wedding. Mr. Ly will probably bring musicians from Phnom Penh."

Without speaking more words, Sreypov left the house and started walking toward Mr. Hang's fields. Ryna followed her. "Don't try to make me marry Kosal," Sreypov said to her mother as they walked side by side. On the other side of the road, Mr. Ly's generator groaned and chugged, partly drowning out the drops of music that dribbled out of the houses.

"I won't," said Ryna. "You should do what you want. I can't speak for your father. He's . . . You know how he is."

"Why do you stay with him?" said Sreypov.

Ryna hesitated. "He's my husband."

"Is that the only reason?" Sreypov turned and looked directly at her mother. Ryna looked away.

"I'm not going to marry Kosal, no matter what," said Sreypov.

Ryna nodded and firmly clasped her daughter's hand. "I know," she said. "Please go talk to your brother about what you should do."

"I know what I'm going to do."

"I mean about your father."

•

Kamal now lived in his own house. A year earlier, shortly after Nita's cremation, he had married a village girl, Han Somrith, and the village men had built the new couple a house near the market. Each morning before dawn, Kamal walked back to the family house, had breakfast with Pich in the dark, yoked the ox under the house, and followed his father to the farm—as he had done since he was fifteen years old.

Sreypov waited for Kamal. When he arrived, trailing a cloud of red dust, he smelled of manure. He invited her into his house, where his wife was chopping vegetables, but Sreypov shook her head no, so they sat on the ground next to the water pump.

"*Bong.* Father wants me to get married," said Sreypov. She noticed that her brother had gained weight since moving into his own house. His cheeks were fuller, and she could see his belly flesh bulging out over his pants. He was taller and bigger than Pich.

"Married to who?"

"Ly Kosal."

"A rich family," said Kamal.

"I'm not doing it," said Sreypov.

Kamal nodded. "Have you talked to Mother?"

"She said talk to you."

Kamal stood up and began walking around the water pump. He was eleven years older than Sreypov, now the man of his own house. As he paced, a wandering chicken hurried to get out of his way and began squawking. "Here's my best advice, Sister," he said. "I think you should ask Father to postpone the marriage for a year. Other things being the same. Then you'll be able to finish school."

"After I finish high school, I'm going to university," said Sreypov. "I'm going to be a poet." Sreypov was no longer certain of these things, but she said them anyway. "Will you speak to Father?"

Kamal looked at his sister in surprise mixed with admiration mixed with fear. "What would I say?" said Kamal.

"You'd say that I should be able to do what I want. You'd say you agree with me. Mother agrees with me."

Kamal's face had turned to stone.

"Father has ruined our family," said Sreypov, loudly enough for Somrith to hear up in the house. She wanted Somrith to hear. "Do you see that, Brother?" Kamal didn't say anything. "You know what he's done. Look how he treats Mother. What he did to Thida. And you. He treats you like cow shit. You wanted to leave Praek Banan. I remember. Why didn't you?"

"Sreypov . . . you're talking about things you don't know."

"I know that you wanted to leave Praek Banan,"

said Sreypov. "I'm not blaming you for that. You should have left. You should have married that girl. What was her name?"

"Sophea."

"Why didn't you marry her?"

Kamal didn't say anything. Finally: "I don't think she wanted to marry me. I wasn't . . ."

"You should have left anyway," said Sreypov. "Father has wrecked our family," she shouted. "I hate him. I hate him."

"Don't say that, Sreypov." Kamal glanced quickly up at his house to see if Somrith had heard anything. In fact, Somrith was standing at the door, worry on her face.

"Yes, I'm saying it. I'm saying it. I hate him. Don't you hate him?"

Kamal put his hand to his brow and began rubbing his forehead back and forth.

"Mother hates him," said Sreypov. "I know she does. She just won't say it. Thida hates him. She won't even look at him. We have to do something."

"What can we do?" said Kamal.

"I don't know," said Sreypov. "You're afraid of him, aren't you."

"I'm not afraid of him."

Sreypov knew he was lying. They were all afraid of Father. "Will you talk to him?"

Kamal sighed. "I'm not sure. You're going so fast with this, Sister. I need to think."

"You know I'm telling the truth."

Kamal stared at the fields across the road. "All right. I'll talk to him."

"When?"

"Sometime in the next couple of weeks. I need to think about what to say. I need to think." Kamal sighed again. He gently touched Sreypov on her shoulder and went up the ladder into his house.

Two new pages in her journal had to be ripped out because they got waterlogged in the fields. On the next page: "12 October 2015: A talk with Brother Kamal last night. He said he would speak to Father and do something. Maybe Father will listen to the other male in the family. But I'm not sure Kamal will do what he said. He doesn't have any spine. Kosal came up to me today at the market and started talking. He's lazy but not stupid. He started telling me all this stuff about his father's moto business and that he was going to inherit the business. He said that once a month he goes with his father to Saigon to work on motos. They own a shop there that fixes the cracked cylinder heads so they can resell the motos. Cracked cylinder heads! Why is he telling me about cracked cylinder heads? Does he think he's getting me to fall in love with him? Does he think cracked cylinder heads are going to make me marry him? I told him that I might write a poem about cracked cylinder heads. He's a nice boy. I hope he finds a wife. Mother is sticking up for me. She should stick up for herself."

For the next week, Pich wasn't feeling well, and Kamal had to work the farm by himself. Pich spent the week mostly hanging around the house, going out occasionally to talk to neighbors who hadn't gone to the fields, complaining of pains in his stomach and back, complaining of getting old. In the house, he continued talking about Sreypov's marriage, but nobody would listen. He didn't bother bathing and started smelling bad, possibly to punish them. "Don't tell me what to do," he snapped at Ryna when she suggested he take a swim in the river to clean off. A couple of nights, he stayed out drinking and came home wrung out and yellow in the face. "Old age," he said. "I never thought I'd be this old." He was fifty-eight.

Sreypov found that she couldn't look at him anymore. Now he had two daughters who wouldn't look at him. Could this go on for the rest of their lives? And she was brooding about what she could do to avoid the marriage. Maybe she could take a bus to Phnom Penh and live with her uncle there. Or maybe something else. The dark thing churned in her stomach.

One late afternoon toward the end of the week, Pich came home with a smile on his face. "I've got some good news," he said. "I talked to Mr. and Mrs. Ly. They give their approval to their son marrying Daughter Sreypov. It will be a great, great wedding. It'll be the greatest wedding that's ever happened in Praek Banan." As he was making this announcement, Sreypov sat on the bamboo floor without looking up, at work on her school lessons, and Ryna and Theary were painting faces on the side of a cardboard box.

Ryna said: "Husband, why did you speak to the Lyses?"

"Why would you ask me such a silly question, *Mae Wea?*" said Pich. "We've been talking about this matter for months now." Pich was sweaty and took off his shirt and dropped it on the floor. "I'm the head of the house," he said. "I make the decisions that are best for the family. This is great news."

"What *you* think is best for the family," said Ryna. "What *you* think. But you know Sreypov doesn't want to get married. What are you doing to your daughters? Our daughters." Ryna was shouting now, a rare thing. Theary started crying, and Thida took her behind the hanging sheet. "What you did to poor Nita," shouted Ryna. "She didn't want to get married. You sent her off to Battambang with that jerk husband. And what you did to Thida. How could you do such a filthy thing to our daughter? I'm not letting you do this to our Sreypov. Never again. She wants to finish high school and to go to university. That's what she's going to do. She'll be the first person in our family to go to university. I wanted to finish high school when I got married. Do you remember? I was fifteen years old. But you said no. You put me to work on the farm. It's not going to happen again. You've ruined two daughters. You're not ruining the third."

As Ryna was shouting, Pich nodded his head slowly, as if hearing out the petty complaints of a child.

Sreypov put her lessons down and stood next to her mother.

Pich pounded his chest. "*I* carry the weight of this family," he said. "Remember that. All of you." He pounded his chest again. "My family goes back four generations in Praek Banan. My grandfather was village chief. *I* could have been village chief if I'd wanted." Thida came back from behind the females' curtain holding Theary in her arms. Pich glanced at her as if she were a fly that had buzzed into the room. "I am the provider. I am the head of the family. The rest of you just complain. Mr. Ly will take care of Sreypov. He'll take care of us, too. I don't deserve to be poor. My family comes from royalty. Remember the plague

on our crops. We barely survived. We're not rich people. Mr. Ly will give our family what we deserve."

"I'd rather be poor," said Thida. She crossed the
room and hugged her mother.

"I'm not getting married," said Sreypov. Was this
the moment? Was this finally the moment to do something? Her hands were shaking, and she could feel
her mother shaking beside her. She felt as if she were
looking at the scene from outside, with every detail
frozen in place—the light streaming through the window behind her father, the women's curtain rippling
slightly in the tiny breeze that blew through the room,
the dark sacks of rice in the corner that looked like old
men squatting on the floor, the smell of the car battery. Was this the moment?

"I'm your father," shouted Pich, "and you'll do
what I tell you."

"No," said Sreypov.

"You're living in my house," shouted Pich.

"I'll go to Phnom Penh. Or I'll move in with
Kamal."

"Kamal does what I tell him."

"I've talked to Kamal," said Sreypov. "He's on my
side."

"I don't believe you."

"Talk to him yourself. I talked to him just a few
days ago."

Pich's face was a fury. Without bothering to put his shirt on, he left the house.

He didn't come back for a week. Thida, Ryna, Sreypov all knew that the earth had tilted, that continents had slid into the sea, perhaps permanently. But the happening was so unfathomable that they couldn't discuss it. So they went about their routines almost in silence—cooking and cleaning, shopping and homework, playing with Theary—as if everything were normal, a pretend normal.

When Pich did return one evening, retching and jaundiced, he was so weak he couldn't climb the ladder. After Ryna helped him up, he sank to the floor. His eyes were yellow and wild. He rolled over and stared at Sreypov. "You've done this to me, Daughter." He doubled up in pain. "You've cursed me. Out there in the night fields. Nobody knows what you do out there. You put a curse on me."

Sreypov glanced at her father writhing on the floor and thought that maybe he was right. Maybe this was the dark thing she'd seen in her mind. Maybe the neighbors had been right all along. She had the bad blood that could not be changed. That night, she buried her blasphemous journal behind the house. But she covered the spot with three rocks so she could find it later if she wanted to.

IV.

I'd like to go to the end of the world,
To explore all that is there,
Also all that is not—
I wouldn't care.
No soil, no wind, no sound,
But beautiful stars all around.

Pich had been lying on his sleeping mat for two weeks, getting thinner and thinner. Everything he ate went right through him. Ryna kept cleaning up his messes and washing his soiled pants. He itched incessantly and sometimes threw off his clothes and scratched until his skin bled. Light bothered him. So the family hung sheets and clothes over the windows and door frame to block out the sun. Loud sounds also annoyed him. So the family kept their voices to whispers. To Sreypov, it didn't seem like a house anymore. They lived in a weird twilight cave. The cave smelled. And her father looked like a strange withered thing. In a daze, she studied her school books by the light of a kerosene lamp. She was certain now that this was the thing that she'd set into motion. But she couldn't see where it was going.

"Maybe you've got a bad case of malaria, or dengue fever," Ryna suggested to Pich. "You'll get better if you can keep the food inside you." "I feel like shit," said Pich. "I'm cursed." He clutched at his stomach and moaned. "I was cursed when I was a kid. Damn them all. My parents said I was the cause of my little sister dying. They said I had thrown out a curse. But it was me who was cursed." He stopped again and held his stomach. "And now I've been cursed again. By my own family." "No one has cursed you," said Ryna, and she massaged Pich's forehead with a wet sponge. Every few minutes, she dipped it into the ointments and herbs brought by the neighbors.

A doctor came from Praek Khmau. He examined Pich and said that it was probably some liver disease, or possibly hepatitis. Auntie Makara offered to pay for Pich to go to a hospital in Phnom Penh, but he was too weak to travel. "When you're feeling better," said Ryna. "These doctors are idiots," said Pich.

Pich began muttering about Sreypov's wedding again. But he wasn't shouting anymore. He was talking backward and forward, like Grandma Lo-la talked. Sreypov figured that if her father got well, it might be the same as before, and she would need to move out of the house. But it probably wouldn't be the same. Look at her father now. He'd shrunk. It wasn't only his body. She could hardly believe what had happened. Only a few weeks ago, her father had been a mountain, and now he was this withered thing who could barely get up from the floor. Yet he was still her father. She wanted to love him, even though she hated him. She knew he'd been poor all his life. She hadn't wanted this to happen, him withered and unable to rise from the floor. She looked at her poor father in the dim light and the stench and couldn't believe what she saw. Her head throbbed.

Kamal came over most evenings and sat on the floor next to Pich, bringing porridge and rubbing balms. He didn't talk about anything except the farm and also some small things going on with him and Somrith. He was managing the farm by himself, he said. Pich heard that and nodded.

Some of Pich's friends also visited—Sayon, Bunrouen, Vitu—one at a time. They gasped when they saw his wasted condition. The room smelled, and there was no ventilation because all the windows and doorway were covered. Nobody could stand visiting more than twenty minutes. "The idiot doctor doesn't know what's wrong with me," said Pich, trying to sit up to greet his friends.

Makara summoned Venerable Khim Ry. The next morning, the old monk laboriously climbed the ladder into the house. For an hour, he chanted prayers. Afterward, he accepted the rice that Ryna offered and put it in his alms bowl.

Another week passed. Pich's cheeks had sunk

and his eyes had receded back in their sockets. On a Tuesday morning, Lakhena arrived. She waited at the bottom of the ladder. "Go away," said Ryna. Lakhena just stood there. Every few minutes, Ryna would go to the doorway, pull the sheets aside, and look to see if Lakhena had gone.

"Who is it?" said Pich.

"Lakhena," said Ryna.

"She shouldn't come here."

"I told her to go away."

After an hour, Ryna went and looked again. Lakhena hadn't moved. Ryna sighed and pulled the sheets aside and beckoned. Lakhena came up the ladder and into the house. When she saw Pich, she winced and sat down beside him. Pich looked at her but didn't say anything.

Lakhena stroked Pich's cheek. She looked around the house. "I've always wondered what your house looked like," she whispered to Ryna. Still with her hand on Pich's cheek, Lakhena turned to Sreypov. "I know that you are taking good care of him," she said.

Sreypov nodded. She didn't know what to say or do with this woman in the house. Then she felt tears on her cheek.

"I love him," said Lakhena.

After a few minutes, Lakhena left. "She shouldn't have come," said Pich.

•

One evening a couple of days after Lakhena's visit, during an especially hot and dry period when the red dust from the road floated up into the house between the poles of the bamboo floor, Pich stopped his crazy muttering, and a calmness came over him. He told Ryna that he was dying. He wanted to say goodbye to the children.

"You aren't dying," said Ryna.

"I know I am," said Pich. "It's my body. I'm dying." He hadn't eaten much of anything since Lakhena's visit. Sreypov listened to him talking in his withered voice and thought to herself that maybe he wanted to die. His power was gone.

"You aren't dying," Ryna said again. They could hear the chanting of a monk just beyond the house. Ryna dabbed at her moist eyes with the corner of her sarong. "You just rest. Would you like to hear some music?" Pich didn't answer. He closed his eyes. "I'd like to play some Sinn Sisamouth," Ryna said. "Very quiet." She turned on the radio and tuned it to the Sinn Sisamouth channel. "We used to listen to Sinn Sisamouth all the time. Do you remember?"

"Yes," said Pich.

"He's an old singer," said Sreypov. She had little interest in Sinn Sisamouth, but she wanted to say something, to be part of the conversation. Something new was happening, and she wanted to be part of it. The man who used to be her father was strangely gone, and there was this new person lying on the floor, a new father. They had a new family, and she wanted to be part of it.

"Old, but good," said Ryna. "Your father likes Sinn Sisamouth. I do too. Is the music OK?" said Ryna. Pich nodded.

A love song ebbed and flowed through the house. The rhythm was deliberate and slow and Sinn's honeyed voice filled with longing. As they listened, Ryna helped her husband turn and lie on his stomach. Then she pulled up his shirt and began rubbing his back with the fifty-riel steel coin she kept in her trunk. She pressed the coin deep into his flesh. He moaned, but it was hard to tell whether it was a moan of pain or the alleviation of pain. "Do you remember when I was sick with pneumonia?" said Ryna. Pich nodded. "You used this same coin on me. This same one." Ryna kept rubbing with the coin, back and forth, back and forth, pushing and pressing until she'd made rows of red bruises on both sides of his back. He moaned again.

"You've been a good wife," Pich whispered. Ryna cradled his cheek, as Lakhena had done. "I blinded my brother," said Pich.

"What are you talking about?" said Ryna.

Pich tried to turn over but didn't have the strength. "Chann, my brother. I jabbed a stick in his eye. I made him blind. He's been living with a cousin in Prey Veng for I don't know how long. He might even be dead by now."

"You're talking crazy talk," said Ryna.

"I did it," said Pich. "I wanted to do it."

"I don't know what you're talking about," said Ryna.

Pich let out a sigh and began turning the fifty-riel steel coin over and over in his hand. "What time is it?" he said.

"Eight."

"I always liked Sinn Sisamouth," said Pich. "I don't know why. My parents listened to him."

"We listened to 'Srolanh Srey Touch' on our first wedding anniversary," said Ryna. "Do you remember?"

"I don't know how you could remember that," said Pich. He had propped himself up on his elbows and was straining to see in the dim light. "Can I talk to Thida? Where's Thida?"

"You need to rest now," said Ryna.

"Thida," Pich said. Thida had been playing with Theary. She put down the toy blocks and stood over her father, turning away from his gaze. She would never forgive him, Sreypov thought to herself. "Thida," he said. "Thida." Thida looked over at her mother. Then she went behind the women's hanging sheet, where she began to cry.

"Where's Sreypov?" said Pich. "Is Sreypov in the house?"

"She's here," said Ryna.

"*Mi-oun*," said Pich.

"Yes," said Sreypov. She sat next to her father. For the first time in nearly a month, she looked into his eyes. And he looked back, a long steady gaze. At that moment, she knew he was dying. Her second father, this man on the floor, was passing away. He turned his body toward her and sighed, his breath heavy. "Daughter." He paused. "Why do you want to go to university?"

Sreypov was startled by the question. For a few moments, she couldn't answer. "I want to continue my studies," she said. Pich stared at her with eyes yellow and still. "The world is big," said Sreypov. "I want to see it."

Pich nodded.

Sreypov dug up her journal, dirt-stained but readable. That night, after returning from the fields, she lay on her sleeping mat, thinking. She could hear her father's heavy breathing, and her mother singing softly to him.

Her father had been sick for six weeks now. He looked like a skeleton. But he didn't seem to be in pain anymore. Perhaps he wouldn't die, after all. Sreypov wanted him to stay alive. She also wanted dear Nita to be alive again. She wanted Thida to forget about the brothel, like it never happened. Was that possible? She wanted her mother to be a star in the sky. Everything was so strange now. *Mae* decided everything. The family was closer now than it ever had been before. At the same time, it didn't feel like a family anymore. It was something new, and changing. They were like pieces of things moving around in the dark. Was it all one accident after another?

Earlier that day, in the market, she'd seen Auntie Makara, who gave her some tea for Father. Auntie Makara said it would make him get well. The leaves of tea were wrapped in a piece of blue paper with a pink string around it. Auntie Makara and Ryna had been friends for forty years. Sreypov tried to imagine her mother forty years ago, when she was a little girl, when she had her whole life ahead of her. Sreypov smiled, but it was a sad smile. She wished that she'd known her mother then, forty years ago. All of that time. Gone, just like that. Most of *Mae*'s life gone, just like that. Sometimes years seem like seconds. Then Sreypov pictured herself in the fields, looking up at the stars. They were so quiet. They saw everything that was going on down here. But they always remained the same.

Notes and Acknowledgments

I am the founder of the Harpswell Foundation, which works to advance a new generation of women leaders in Cambodia and all of Southeast Asia.

In connection with this project, I have gone to Cambodia twice a year since 2003. For help in vetting the manuscript for cultural accuracy, I thank Limheang Heng, Donald Jameson, Menghun Kaing, Kalyanee Mam, Socheata Poeuv, Savada Prom, and Kem Sos. For editorial help, I thank George Kovach, Yael Goldstein Love, Betsy Sallee, and my wonderful editor at Counterpoint Press, Dan Smetanka.

ALAN LIGHTMAN is the author of six novels, including the international bestseller *Einstein's Dreams*, as well as *The Diagnosis*, a finalist for the National Book Award. He is also the author of a memoir, three collections of essays, and several books on science. His work has appeared in *The Atlantic, Granta, Harper's Magazine, The New Yorker, The New York Review of Books, Salon, Nature,* and *Nautilus,* among other publications. He has taught at Harvard and at MIT, where he was the first person to receive a dual faculty appointment in science and the humanities. In 2003, Lightman founded the Harpswell Foundation, a nonprofit organization whose mission is to empower a new generation of women leaders in Cambodia and Southeast Asia. He lives in the Boston area.